Below the Border

"They call me *el Cabrito* down here," the Kid said.

Charro laughed. "You—*el Cabrito*? The man whose rifle never misses, who moves like a ghost, who handles a knife better than any man in Mexico? You mean to tell us that *you* are *el Cabrito*?"

Ysabel unbuckled his gunbelt and pulled an eleven-inch Bowie from his boot.

"I will give you proof," he said. "We will go into that canebrake thirty yards apart. Only one of us will come out. Will that satisfy you?"

J.T. Edson

THE YSABEL KID

CHARTER BOOKS, NEW YORK

This Charter book contains the
complete text of the original edition.
It has been completely reset in a typeface
designed for easy reading and was printed
from new film.

THE YSABEL KID

A Charter Book/published by arrangement with
Transworld Publishers, Ltd.

PRINTING HISTORY
Corgi edition published 1968
Berkley edition / August 1978
Charter edition / September 1989

ISBN: 1-55773-273-6

Charter Books are published by The Berkley Publishing Group,
200 Madison Avenue, New York, N.Y. 10016.
The name "CHARTER" and the "C" logo are
trademarks belonging to Charter Communications, Inc.

PRINTED IN THE UNITED STATES OF AMERICA

10 9 8 7 6 5 4 3 2 1

For Linda Hyde
my favourite librarian

THE YSABEL KID

CHAPTER ONE

Bring Back Bushrod Sheldon

"BRING BACK BUSHROD SHELDON!"

That was the order President U.S. Grant gave so lightly, back in Washington. It was however an order that would not be so easy to carry out, and that General Philo Handiman knew in every campaign-toughened inch of his body.

The Civil War was over and had been for a year or more now. With peace the Government in Washington was turning its attention to the problem of Mexico where the French usurper, Maximillian, ruled the country with the bayonets and sabres of his troops and Benito Juarez fought back with the savagery of one possessed.

The United States gave long consideration to the matter for they did not want a European controlled country on each flank of their young and fast growing nation. The decision to lend help to Juarez came after long argument. Canada was firm under the distant Grandmother so the United States looked south. There was a large, well armed, equipped and battlewise army ready to move.

Then someone remembered old Bushrod Sheldon.

Sheldon was a hard-headed, hard-fighting Southern gentleman who refused calmly to accept Robert E. Lee's decision to end the useless killing. Disdaining to surrender he went south to join Maximillian and fight Juarez.

Now one cantankerous old Dixie soldier would hardly have made such a great difference to the plans of a nation, but when he went two hundred and fifty fire-eating warriors as tough and battlewise as any the Union Army could show went with him.

Even so they would merely have been a drop in the ocean compared with the number of men the United States was prepared to release from Indian fighting and garrison duties. In numbers that is. General Handiman, head of the newly formed Secret Service, got word through his agents in the South that if Sheldon was attacked by Union troops every half-reconstructed Rebel would dig up the Appomattox-buried hatchet and paint once more for war.

This provoked serious discussion in the Capital, and there were varied views on what would be the best course to follow. The ''Boy General,'' now no more than a very junior Lieutenant-Colonel, George Armstrong Custer was one who raised his voice for open war and to hell with the consequences. However, war was his kind's only answer to every problem.

Saner heads, reviewing the casualty list in the Union Army caused by fighting those hardy sons of the South, agreed that Sheldon must be brought back. Even if it meant offering some fair-sized concessions to get him to return. The only serious problem after making the decision was whether the old-timer would come back. One thing was for sure. Bushrod Sheldon would never return on the word of a Yankee.

Finally, after much long thought President Grant dropped the handling of the affair into General Handiman's lap and let it lie there. Handiman knew that there was one man who might get Bushrod Sheldon to return. But would that man help?

Handiman eased himself in the uncomfortable seat of the Army buggy and let his aide get on with the driving without any comment or conversation. In fact Handiman hadn't done much talking since they left Washington headed for the cattle country of South West Texas, headed to visit the man Handiman thought might be able to talk sense to Bushrod Sheldon.

Ole Devil Hardin was just as tough, hard and irascible and as loyal to the stars and bars of Dixie as Sheldon and could talk as an old and trusted friend to the other man. If Hardin would help that is.

In the days before the war Handiman had been a friend and welcome to the great OD Connected ranch but Ole Devil Hardin wore Confederate grey in the War and led the Texas Light Cavalry Brigade. It all hinged on his decision to forget the War and go down there into trouble-torn Mexico to take Grant's letter and his own sage advice to Sheldon.

Handiman remembered how after the Appomattox Ole Devil Hardin turned his Brigade back to Texas and disbanded those hardy, battlewise young veterans and left word that as far as the Rio Hondo country was concerned reconstruction was out and no Yankee need show his face there. It said much for the esteem the Texas Light Cavalry's commander was held in for no Union soldiers had been near his area since the War.

Lieutenant Collings, Handiman's aide, had not held his post for six months without learning when he could be expected to make polite conversation and when to keep his mouth clamped tight shut. This was one of the latter times, the General was worried and deep in thought; he wouldn't take it kindly having his thoughts interrupted. So Collings was free to relax and let the two-horse team follow the rough wagon trail with a minimum of bother. He was free to look around the miles of rolling Texas range country, grazing lands of the OD Connected and the Barbed B ranches. Looking up a slope he saw something which made him break the silence and risk Handiman's anger.

"How far are we from the ranch, sir?" he asked.

"About five miles," Handiman replied, pleased that the young man had broken the silence and his worries could be forgotten for a time.

"Then there will be no danger from those Indians?"

"Indians?" Handiman was hardly concentrating at the moment. "Which Indians?"

"Up there on the rim!"

Handiman twisted round and squinted his eyes as he looked up the slope. He saw which Indians were meant. They sat there lining the top of a rim overlooking the trail. Twenty squat built, savage faced young braves, naked to the waist and everyone of them holding a lance. This apart from the knives or tomahawks at their belts were their only weapons.

Studying the Indians Handiman realised they were the first hostiles he'd seen in many years. In fact, he'd not fought Indians since back in forty-seven when Sam Colt's first model Dragoon revolver was being debated as a new-fangled contraption which would ruin the conception of the mounted soldier. What this amounted to was that man did not know much about Indians in general and Comanches in particular.

With more knowledge he'd have been far more worried than he was now. Ordinary Comanches were bad enough, these were not ordinary Comanches. They were of the Dog Soldier Lodge. Twenty of those bad hat, war wise young warriors were more than a match for an equal number of Indian fighting trained soldiers. No two officers, fresh shone bright and out of Washington, would stand a chance of survival against them.

"Move that team!" Handiman barked. "We'll have to run for it."

The aide swung his whip to crack it in the air, that was all the two horses needed to know. They lunged forward into the traces hard enough to lift the buggy clear off the ground. When it lit down again the wheels were spinning fast and the team running.

That was where Handiman made his first mistake. The comanches were here on a scouting mission and not after war, yet like animals they bore the instinct to pursue anything which ran from them. This was too good a chance to miss. A pair of bluecoat soldiers alone and unescorted would be easy meat and would provide trophies to take back to the lodges of the tribe. With the thought of this and showing the superb horsemanship which made them the equal of any light cavalry in the world the Comanches sent their horses in a rumpscraping slide down the slope headed for the trail.

"No bows or rifles," Handiman growled to his aide. "That's luck."

It wasn't the kind of luck a man knowledgeable in Indian ways would have wanted. Those lances told a grim and dangerous story. It meant the Comanches were under lodge oath to count coup with the lance and would press an attack even after their brothers armed with bow and rifle were all done and headed for home.

The braves hit the trail about thirty yards behind the buggy and hurled their wiry war ponies after it. Handiman watched them and then pulled out his Colt 1860 Army revolver, earing back the hammer. He held his fire, waiting for a better chance than was yet made for it took time to remove the spent caps from the nipples and recharge each separate chamber with powder and ball. There was no time to spare.

Handiman lined his gun and fired at the nearest brave. Even at that range the bullet must have come close for the young man ducked in an involuntary move which brought derisive cheers from his friends. He straightened and howled out his kill or die shout, then sent his horse forward even faster.

In his time at the Point, Collings had been known as one of the finest racing buggy drivers. His team today were as good as could be selected by a Major with an eye on promotion and desire to please the General, but harnessed horse was never sired that could pull a buggy and outrun Comanche war-ponies urged on by name-making braves after white-eye scalps. The team tried its best but those screaming young warriors drew nearer with every raking, ground covering stride.

Carefully, Handiman fired two more shots, but neither took effect, his fourth shot sent a wild-eyed brave rolling in the churned up dust but the others kept right straight on. This was a disappointment to the General for he'd hoped that losing a man would turn the others off. He didn't know Dog Soldiers, they could count well and knew just how many bullets a revolver carried, so were waiting for two more to be fired. In the rocking buggy Handiman reached over and removed his aide's Colt, knowing that the young man could not handle reins and gun. He felt slightly better with a gun in each hand for he could now turn loose eight chunks of lead and he hoped to make some of it count.

Behind, the Comanches sent their racing ponies surging forward, not following any set plan of attack but all racing to be the first to count coup. This was their usual method of fighting and gave Handiman some slight advantage for the young braves got in each other's way. Then one lunged forward, ahead of the other wild riders. The Colt lined on him but just as Handiman fired the brave slipped over one flank and hung there causing the bullet to miss him and knock a man behind from his racing pony.

The other braves were closing in now and regretfully Handiman shot the nearest horse from under him. The brave lit down running and as a riderless pony went by in the wake of the others caught it by the mane and vaulted aboard.

It was the aide who first saw dust rising ahead of them, he yelled and tried to attract Handiman's attention to it. The General only managed to give one quick glance, then turned his attention back to the Indians behind. The dust ahead must mean the Comanches had friends there and it looked as if Handiman's task was coming to an abrupt end.

Up on the rim the dustcloud rolled, hard riding shapes now showing in it. A yell shattered the air and Handiman heard it with relief though he'd never thought to be pleased to hear that sound. It was the wild ringing Rebel battlecry he'd heard at Shilo, Bull Run, Antietam; heard it and cursed it. Now it was the sweetest and most pleasant sound in the world.

Eight hard riding men came tearing down the slope, riding with the same skill as the Comanches showed earlier. The man in the centre of the group gave a shouted order and the eight cowhands fanned out like a well trained cavalry. This was not in itself surprising for the Rio Hondo had stripped its lands of young men to fight in the Texas Light Cavalry Brigade.

Collings' attention was taken from the sight of those men by the sight of a Comanche brave, lance lowered to kill the offside horse, riding alongside. Lashing out with the buggy whip Collings felt it bite into the brown skin and the brave jerked his horse out of range. But the others were crowding in, all wanting to get to the buggy and count coup before the guns of the cowhands drove them off.

The cowhands were coming in fast, their leader barked another order and their revolvers came clear but he did not take his white-handled Colt 1860 Army guns from their butt forward holsters. He sat that huge paint stallion like a centaur and watched with calculating eyes the distance closing. Then his hands crossed and the sun reflected dully on the blued frames of the guns as they came out.

Handiman was in bad trouble. Two braves were close in to the wagon, one at either side. The General knew that he could only get one of the two. If he killed the man lining on him the young Lieutenant would die. If he killed the other, the man nearest him would send the lance crashing into him. Ahead on the trail the cowhands were bringing their horses into line and charging on though they were all holding their fire. Handiman did not see them; he made his decision. Collings was a young man and a useful officer. With this in mind Handiman brought his gun round to save the young officer's life. Then he heard what he thought was one shot and the man on his right went down over the back of his horse while the other at the left swayed over with lead in him.

Smoke curled up from the matched guns in the hands of the leader of the cowhands. He'd fired both so near together that the two shots sounded as one. Then in echo of his shots the other men fired as smooth a volley as it had ever been General Handiman's pleasure to hear. The Comanches rocked back visibly under that volley, three went down but the rest pressed home their attack on both buggy and cowhands.

Dust clouds whirled round and through the dust Handiman got brief glimpses of the wild battle around him. He saw a wild-eyed brown face looming up and sent a bullet into it. Then for a brief instant the cowhand on the paint came into view, he seemed to have eyes which saw all round him and guns that lined themselves.

Then it was over, the Comanches whirled their horses, the ten who were left, and raced off fast. Even travelling as they did only one body was left behind by the fleeing braves, the rest had been scooped up and carried off.

The dust cloud rolled away and the grinning cowhands sat their horses around the buggy. One of their number was dabbing a lance slash on his leg and the rest of them crowded round making ribald comments about him.

"Get after them!" Collings yelled angrily. "Chase them—"

"Sure thing, soldier boy," a lean grinning cowhand agreed.

"Like hell," the man on the big paint stallion replied softly as the other riders started to turn their horses. "You bunch have work to do. You're not Army, getting paid to fight Indians."

"They warn't fighting Indians Cap'n," the hand objected. "Were running away from them, way I saw it."

Collings snorted angrily; he was used to civilians treating him with some respect. He pointed after the fast disappearing braves and snapped: "Why don't you allow the men to follow them. Find out where they're going and teach them a further sharp lesson."

"Mister," the small man on the paint looked Collings over with a cold, icy disgust the Lieutenant hadn't seen since his first year as a plebe at West Point, the look a senior cadet gave to a junior who made silly suggestions. "When a Comanche Dog Soldier lights out like that not even a Texan can catch up with them. Likewise we know where they're going. If we try to inflict further lessons on them, where they're going they've got friends who'll inflict it right back again."

Handiman studied the small man who appeared to be in command of the riders. That other hand had called him "Cap'n," it must be either a nickname or used in a mocking sense. If he was giving orders it meant he was in all probability one of Ole Devil's kin. That would explain why they took his orders. There could be no other reason why grown men would obey so insignificant a youngster.

He wasn't a tall man, this leader. Nor could he show such a

commanding figure as the tall, heavily built General. His black J.B. Stetson hat was thrust back to show his curly, dusty blond hair. His face was handsome enough, a young face with grey eyes which looked hard at a man and met the gaze without flinching. Around his throat was a tight rolled bandana of red silk, the ends hanging long over his dark red shirt. The jean overalls were faded and the cuffs turned back, hanging loose over his expensive, fancy decorated boots. Around his waist was a hand-tooled gunbelt with a Confederate Army buckle and in the holsters of the belt were the matched brace of bone-handled Colt revolvers he'd used so well; they looked out of place on so young a frame, for the rider did not look older than sixteen or so. That paint stallion, too, was as fine an animal as it had been Handiman's pleasure to look on. Yet the small young man did not look as if he should own or be riding so fine a creature.

The small man twisted in his cow horned, double girthed Texas range saddle and spoke to the others. "You bunch head back there to the herd. Uncle Devil'll likely be fit to be tied if we haven't finished branding and earmarking them by tonight."

The other riders did not appear to object to this young man giving them orders but that was understandable. If he was kin of Ole Devil Hardin and the old timer told them to work under him then they would work. Ole Devil was the owner of a temper which was, to say the least, sulphurous and a flow of language that would not disgrace the best efforts of a thirty-year top-sergeant of Cavalry who'd been learning from a bullwhacker. That same temper and language would be turned full loose and with all his power on the head of any man who tried to make a fool of anyone Ole Devil chose to act as his deputy.

The small rider turned his attention back to the two Army officers after he'd watched the other men headed back in the way they'd come. His eyes were neither friendly nor subservient as he watched them and asked: "You wanting something in these parts?"

Handiman could hardly expect this coldness and lack of

hospitality on the part of the young man. The war had been over for a year and although the rest of Texas was writhing under the heel of the reconstructionists, the Rio Hondo country was left strictly alone. Handiman was no even tempered mild mannered man himself. The Army was not an easy school and did not tend to breed mild mannered saints. However, for once in his life he held down the anger which boiled up in him. It would do neither him nor President Grant's business any good to bawl out this small youngster who appeared to be quite a favourite with Ole Devil Hardin if his position of trust was anything to go by.

"We've come to visit Ole Devil," he explained.

"That'll make his day," there was a mocking note in that soft-drawled voice.

Lieutenant Collings' face turned red with anger. He'd been just too young to fight in the war but was full of the propriety of and the superiority of an officer in the Union Army when dealing with a Southerner. "This is General Handiman," he snapped angrily. "You ought—"

"Spread's that way. I'll ride along in with you and make sure you don't get lost," the Texan replied, he looked around, glancing back in the way the buggy had come. "You lose many men?"

"None," Handiman answered, silencing his aide's angry outburst before it could even start. "We came alone."

The small Texan glanced at Handiman's face and looked around again. It was not the usual thing for a full General of the Union Army to travel around in Texas without a sizeable escort. Particularly if he was coming to the OD Connected on the business the Texan suspected.

"All right, we can get going then," there was still no friendship or even any interest in the voice.

Handiman nodded to the aide who clucked to the team and started them forward at an easy walk. Handiman watched the young man riding alongside the buggy and tried to decide which of the three Rio Hondo families he belonged to. It was hard to say for the Hardin, Blaze and Fog men were all tallish men and this small, unassuming young man didn't feature any of the clan Handiman knew.

The trail made a long, looping curve round the foot of the slope and at the far side Handiman found himself looking over a fair sized herd of cattle held by fast moving riders. Near at hand was the chuckwagon set up with a tall, grizzled old-timer just preparing food for the hands. At the far side of the herd, where much of the activity was taking place, the smoke from the branding fires rose to be dispersed by the wind before it cleared the rim.

The scene was one of feverish activity, cattle moved restlessly while the cowhands spun and raced their horses round oblivious of dust and noise. It was a scene that would be being repeated across the Texas range as the great cattle herds were gathered for the spring round-up.

Handiman looked around him. It was difficult with the churned up dust to see any of the riders on the herd plainly but one thing he was sure of. Ole Devil Hardin was not there with the men. This in itself was unusual and something Handiman wasn't expecting, for Hardin lived by the maxim of never telling a man to do what he couldn't do himself.

"Isn't Ole Devil out here?" he asked.

"Nope," The Texan was watching the herd work too, listening to the distant cry of "More straw," as some brander shoved his branding iron into a fire which was not blazing enough to meet his approval.

"Never thought he'd be at the house when there was work out here to be done with his herd," Handiman remarked, for there was no need to conceal the fact that he knew Ole Devil really well. It might change this small youngster's attitude if he knew that the Yankee General was an old friend of the family.

Once more the young man turned in his saddle and looked back along the trail in a suspicious manner. Handiman wasn't sure if this was natural caution or if the Texan thought Handiman did bring an escort and had either sacrificed or lost all of them to the Comanches, or they'd run away. Handiman wondered why the Texan expected him to bring an escort on a peaceful visit to an old friend.

"Ole Devil ill or something?" Handiman asked as the Texan showed no sign of explaining the rancher's absence.

"You mean you haven't heard?" the Texan's face almost showed surprise as he started the paint forward again.

"Heard what?"

"Ole Devil came off a bad hoss. Got piled and hurt bad."

There was a sudden cold feeling came over Handiman's stomach as he looked at the small young man. "Is he hurt bad?"

"Tied down in a wheelchair. He'll likely never walk again."

CHAPTER TWO

Ole Devil's Segundo

GENERAL HANDIMAN gripped the sides of the wagon, clutching until the knuckles showed white. It was a bitter pill to swallow, coming all these miles, wasting valuable time and then finding the one man he thought could help him crippled and tied to a wheelchair. Grant would be furious at the delay and the men who thought the Secret Service a waste of money would have further proof that they were correct.

The small Texan did not carry on speaking, he just held the paint to an easy walk, his cold, unfriendly eyes constantly checking on the back trail. Handiman was also in no talkative mood, even though he was curious to know who the young man was. He sat hunched in the seat looking mean and angry. From the corner of his eye he saw his aide open his mouth to say something, then close it again, the words unsaid.

They were still silent as the ranch came into view as they topped a rim. Hardiman looked down at a place he would never forget, the place where his career met with its most outstanding failure. That was all this trip would be accounted in the records. He'd delayed the start of the Mexican business to come down here and obtain Ole Devil Hardin's help. The help would not be forthcoming now, could not be if the old man was crippled.

The ranch house was a long, two-storey stone building which looked strong enough to be, and was, a fort in times when the Comanche raiders came sweeping down in search

13

of war. At the right flank of the house stood the bunkhouse and cookshack, effectively covering one side of the house while being covered by it. At the other side, also stone built were the stables, store-sheds and a large building used as a dancehall when the guests of Ole Devil's Christmas turkeyshoot came. At other times it served as a repository for saddles and other various gear. Out beyond the ranch, backing right up to the Rio Hondo stood the blacksmith's shop, its forge sending up smoke as a man worked in it. In front of the building were three pole corrals, the one at the right with a snubbing post in the centre and empty, the other two with a scattering of horses and ponies. The main remuda would be out with the herd and the other saddlestock grazing on the range.

The reason for the ponies became clear as the buggy came nearer. It was holiday time in the Rio Hondo country and the children from the various families of the clan were out at the spread. A dozen or so boys ranging from eight to thirteen were playing in the empty corrals but they stopped and ran to climb the fences and watch the buggy coming nearer. Then as the small Texan brought his horse to a halt they swarmed over the rail with yells of delight and crowded round, asking to be allowed to walk the big animal.

The small man laughed and tossed the reins to one of the older boys, then told two more to attend to the visitor's rig. This did not meet with approval from any of the youngsters and Handiman managed to grin at some of the comments about their having to take care of horses for a couple of damned Yankee blue-bellies. Yet they obeyed this small man without further question. That would be because they knew he was Ole Devil's favourite. The eagerness to walk the horse came from the Rio Hondo boys' love for fine animals and the paint was all of that.

"Ole Devil's just come on the porch," the Texan told Handiman, indicating the house with a jerk of his head. "I surely hope you know what you are doing."

"I reckon I do," Handiman answered. He was still at a loss to explain the young man's attitude. He did not look old enough to have been in the War and gave the impression of being too intelligent to bear a grudge against a soldier who'd only done his duty by fighting for his beliefs.

"Dustine!" Ole Devil's voice was the same as when Handiman last heard it. Hard, sharp and meant to be obeyed instantly. "What the hell are those blue bellies doing here."

"You're getting blind, you old goat," Handiman yelled back before the Texan could speak. "And the War ended in sixty-five."

Ole Devil Hardin leaned forward in the wheelchair and squinted, then he gave a yell back. "What the—By cracky, it's you Philo. Come on up here."

Handiman walked across the open space followed by his Aide and the small man. The General took his time and looked his old friend over. The face was the same, sharp, tanned and aristocratic. Coal black eyes piercing and level gazed, a hooked nose and a hard, grim fighting man's mouth. The Confederate General's coat hung loose over his wheelchair. Only the tartan blanket round his legs showed that he was crippled and would never walk again.

Behind Hardin stood a small, smiling man with an Oriental cast of features which made the cowhands think he was Chinese. He was Tommy Okasi, Ole Devil's servant and he insisted that he was really Nipponese, whoever that might be. Ole Devil found him in New Orleans, where a clipper-ship brought and left him. The small man came back west with Ole Devil and settled down in the Rio Hondo where his small size and Oriental mien might have found him being bullied if he hadn't been well versed in a strange fighting technique which rendered helpless even the biggest and strongest men.

"Get some burgundy, Tommy," Ole Devil ordered as he shook Handiman's hand and looked his friend over. "Didn't recognise you with all that shining brasswork, Philo, and you're getting as fat as a hawg." He glared at his servant who hadn't moved. "Where's the burgundy?"

"Betty San told me no burgundy for you in daytime. She make me one time sick Nippon feller she hears I give it to you."

"Betty's back East," Old Devil barked back. "She'll never know."

The small Texan came up on to the porch after the others and sat on the rail, swinging his legs idly. He looked Handiman over for a long moment then remarked, "I thought it was strange, a full-blowed Yankee general coming here looking for Cousin Wes and without an escort."

Handiman got it now, although his aide was still puzzled. It explained the young man's animosity and his careful surveying of the range as he rode alongside the buggy. Handiman laughed: "You thought I was hunting for Wes Hardin?"

Then Collings got it. John Wesley Hardin, Ole Devil's nephew, was being hunted by the Army for killing a drunken negro who attacked him. The young Texan thought this was what brought General Handiman here and so showed caution and escorted him to the ranch to prevent him going anywhere he shouldn't. Collins scanned the range and wondered if even now Wes Hardin might be watching them over the sights of rifle, primed and ready for trouble.

"Didn't really think you'd be fool enough to try it alone," the Texan went on. "But like Uncle Devil always says—"

"I can imagine, son," Handiman interrupted, his tones more friendly now. Then he turned his attentions back to Ole Devil. "You being stove up this way puts me in a hell of a spot."

"How come?"

"I've been sent from Washington by Sam Grant. He wants you to do something for him, something real important."

"Well now, does he?" Ole Devil's frosty black eyes glinted at the thought of President U.S. Grant wanting his help so badly as to send the head of his Secret Service after it. "Old Sam must be getting pretty close to the blanket if he's sent for me to help him."

"We needed you badly," Handiman agreed as he looked down at the blankets covering Ole Devil's lower regions. "How did this happen?"

Ole Devil jerked an expressive thumb to where the boy

was leading the big paint stallion round in front of the corral. "See that paint there. Finest piece of hossflesh I've bought in years, a real good hoss. Young Dustine here handles it real well. I tried."

Handiman looked with renewed interest at the small young man. He might be young and not look much at all but he must be a horseman if he could trim and break the mount which threw and crippled the South's greatest horsemaster, Ole Devil Hardin.

"It leaves me in a hell of a hole," Handiman remarked, wondering if he shoud tell Hardin why he'd come here and yet not wanting to say too much about it in front of his aide and a small man.

"Best tell me about it then," Hardin answered.

Handiman coughed and looked at the small Texan who still lounged on the rail. "How about showing Mr. Collings here round the ranch house?" he asked.

"Sorry, I just came in to see you didn't get lost. I haven't time to act as guide for your boy," the Texan swung down from the porch and jerked his hand towards the door. "Get Tommy to show him into the study, the guns might interest him. I'm going to the cookshack, Uncle Devil, Jimmo sent his louse in after breakfast and hasn't seen hide nor hair of him since."

Handiman offered his cigar case to Ole Devil and watched the young man walk away, then directed Collings to go and look over the collection of firearms which decorated the walls of Ole Devil's study. Then with the porch cleared and the cigars going started to tell what brought him here. Ole Devil sat back, relaxed and enjoying his smoke, but he was listening with care and attention. When the talking was done he gave his opinion:

"Bushrod won't come back."

"I'd agree with you if it wasn't for this letter from Grant. I hoped that you could take it and talk to him."

"I might at that," Hardin agreed. "You say you've got that letter from Grant with you?"

"Sure," Handiman patted his pocket where the thick letter

for Bushrod Sheldon bulged it. "It gives so many concessions that it only needs one more to say the South won after all."

"All right then," Ole Devil replied. "I'll get it delivered for you. Tommy!" This last was in a yell which brought the servant from the house. "Go get Dusty."

Handiman watched the small servant hurrying across towards the cookshack but didn't connect anything yet. He shook his head: "Bushrod won't listen to anyone except you."

"Won't he?" Hardin replied stubbing out the cigar. "He'll listen to the man I send. He'll listen because I'm going to send him a message and a letter. And anyway he'd listen to the man I'm sending."

The small Texan came back with Tommy Osaki, looking even younger with his hat in his hand. "You needing me, Uncle Devil?" he asked.

"Hold hard, Devil," Handiman snapped, hardly noticing his aide had emerged from the house and was standing behind him. "This is a dangerous and very important mission and—"

"I know that," Ole Devil snapped back. "That's why I'm sending Dusty here. Do you think I'd be sending my segundo right in the middle of the spring round-up if it wasn't? Was it less important I'd get one of the Blaze twins to go." Then he stopped and a grin creased his face as he watched Handiman's face. "Reckon I must have forgotten to introduce you. This is my nephew, Dusty Fog."

Handiman's cigar fell from his hand, his mouth dropped open and he stared for a second at the small man. He'd heard that name before, so had his aide and it was the latter who spoke:

"Captain Dusty Fog of the Texas Light Cavalry?"

"Retired," the small man replied.

The name meant something to both of them, yet neither would have ever connected it with this small insignificant looking man. It meant that here stood one of the South's supreme trio of raiders, ranking with Turner Ashby and John Singleton Mosby. It mean hard riding, hard hitting men striking like Comanches and disappearing again before the Union forces could organise either defence or pursuit. It meant even more. This small, young man caused more than one professional Yankee soldier to curse impotently and wish he was fighting a more conventional opponent.

Things were more clear now to Handiman. Back there when that cowhand called Dusty Fog "Cap'n" it was respect and not derision. Handiman should have known that those reckless sons of the saddle never gave their respect to a man for who his kin were but for what he himself was. It was the same with the young boys out there. It was respect for their hero which prompted them to crowd round and ask to be allowed to handle his horse.

"I owe you an apology," Captain Handiman remarked as he held out his hand. "I didn't recognise you. But you'll do the job if any man can."

"What job is that?" Dusty asked, looking from his uncle to the General.

"I want you to go into Mexico and bring back Bushrod Sheldon," Handiman explained. "You're the only one who could do it now Ole Devil is out."

"I'll try, but I know Bush Sheldon. He'll not come."

"He'll come when he reads this letter from President Grant."

"I'd sooner take him smallpox. It'd make me more popular with him," Dusty growled.

Handiman smiled, this young man certainly knew Bushrod Sheldon. "You'd better read the letter," he said and passed over the envelope.

Pulling open the flap Dusty opened the large sheet of paper and read it through. At the end he looked at Handiman and asked: "They want him back this badly?"

"They want him back that bad."

Dusty whistled as he thought over the concessions made in that letter. He looked at the letter, then at his uncle. Ole Devil reached out a hand, took the letter and read it through. He folded the paper, put it back into the envelope once more and grunted: "It won't be easy."

"I won't," Handiman agreed. "Juarez won't know who you are and his men have a nasty way of shooting gringos first then asking questions. The French may know we're sening a man, and if they do they'll move heaven and earth to stop you reaching Bushrod Sheldon."

"That figgers," Dusty replied, although he didn't appear unduly alarmed at it.

"Do you speak French or Spanish?"

"Speak saddle Mex and a mite of French, can get by in either."

"Good, it'll be a help. Now Washington is trying to arrange for a man to go along with you as far as the Juaristas, I'd like you to go with him. There was a mixup over this and I don't know who he is, or anything about him. He will be in Brownsville, Cameron County until the end of the week of so, waiting to contact the Juarez men. I'd like you to locate him and go with him."

Dusty wasn't too keen on this idea. He would much prefer to go alone, or if he needed help to take his now retired Top-sergeant, Billy Jack, or his cousin Red Blaze along. They were men he could trust, tried and found not wanting in either brains or courage.

"I'd rather go it alone," he replied for both Red and Billy Jack were needed here in Texas.

"The man won't go far with you. Only to the Juarez men," Handiman replied. "Will you do it?"

Dusty looked at Ole Devil. The old man nodded imperceptibly and Dusty said, "Sure. I'll head for home and pick up some gear I'll need."

"Come back for dinner, boy," Ole Devil called as Dusty stepped from the porch and walked away. "We've got things to talk over."

Hondo Fog, Sheriff of Rio Hondo County, watched his son riding towards the house in Polveroso City. He noted Dusty was afork a speed horse left behind when the crew took the remuda as being too fast for cattlework. So Hondo went along the path through the flower garden and opened the gate.

"Ole Devil fired you, son?" he asked.

"Could call it that," Dusty replied as he swung down from the saddle and tied the horse up. "He wants me to head south of the border for him."

Hondo Fog asked no questions, but he knew that Mexico was no place for an ex-Confederate officer to be riding these days. The sheriff made quite a contrast to his son, for Hondo Fog stood well over six foot tall, was wide shouldered and powerful looking.

They entered the living room and Hondo hung his Confederate officer's hat on a peg, then turned and looked down at his son. Before he could ask any questions the door opened and Mrs. Fog came in. She was a tall, plump, smiling woman with the black eyes of a Hardin, yet softer and gentler than Ole Devil's.

"You look hungry boy," she said. "I won't be sorry when young Betty comes back from the East. She makes Jimmo serve up better than his everlasting son-of-a-gun stew."

Dusty grinned. His cousin Betty made other things happen at the ranch when she was there. She was only his age, just under twenty, but she ruled that spread with a rod of iron.

"I have to head back as soon as I can, maw," he replied. "Just came to collect some of my gear. I'd like my uniform packing in my warbag."

"Uniform?"

"Yes'm. That's the way I'm going to have to handle this."

"Sounds real important, son," Hondo remarked, knowing that the OD Connected were in the middle of their spring roundup and that Dusty was the roundup captain.

"Some," Dusty agreed, taking a chair and as his father sat down telling him of his mission. "Could be bad if General Bushrod won't come back."

"Could be," Hondo was an old campaigner and full fed up with the horror of a war which set brother to killing brother. He looked to where above the fireplace a pair of crossed sabres hung below a bullet torn Cavalry pennant. "You want your sabre?"

"Not this time," Dusty answered regretfully for he had

the true cavalry regard for the sabre as a fighting weapon. "I couldn't hide it until I needed it. I'll take a rifle if I can."

Hondo waved a hand towards the stand of long arms in the corner of the room and Dusty went towards them, looking them over. The single-shot, muzzling loading weapons he dismissed right away. The old Colt revolving breech rifle did not meet with his approval either. That left two choices, either a Henry rifle or a Spencer carbine. Both were repeaters and yet neither really were what he wanted in a saddlegun. The Henry was too heavy and long for comfortable saddle use and also prone to jam up if the long tube magazine was knocked against anything. The Spencer was more the length, but too heavy in calibre at .56 to be really easy in use from a horse.

"Take the Spencer if I can," he said, looking down at the engraving on the lock.

It read: "1st New York Vols.", a regiment neither Dusty nor his father served in nor did anything other than shoot at. The carbine and the Henry were battlefield captures, taken in the War.

Hondo Fog went to the saddleboot belonging to the Carbine and Dusty unlocked a box in the corner. From it he took two wooden boxes each containing ten tubes of seven bullets for the Spencer carbine. Two cardboard boxes of Colt Combustible cartridges came next, then a buckskin bag holding ready moulded bullets and a mould to make more. Lastly he took a couple of powder flasks, one a plain horn, the other belonging to his matched brace of guns, complete with a measure to give the correct weight of powder for the chambers of the guns.

He took the pile of ammunition into the bedroom where his mother was carefully folding his cadet grey Confederate uniform with the Captain's braid at the sleeve cuffs and the triple bars of half-inch wide, three-inch long gold braid at the collar.

"You'll be back soon, son?" she asked as she put the uniform into the war bag and placed a couple of clean shirts on top of it.

"I'll try. I'd best get back before Betty comes home or I'll be in bad trouble. That ole paint of mine got into her truck garden and surely mussed it up. I want to see that it's straightened out before she gets back."

Mrs. Fog watched her small, soft spoken son with eyes that were bright with pride and unshed tears. She was worried at his going on so dangerous a mission but knew that few men were better equipped to do it. She'd seen him ride to war in the footsteps of his father and uncle at fifteen and then return at eighteen a Captain and a hero. Then she'd seen him go west to help another uncle, Colonel Charles Goodnight, in the first of the early cattledrives after the War, drives which were to set the pattern and bring money pouring into Texas for the next few years.

She'd faith in this small son, her elder son, and knew that he would return to the Rio Hondo country.

Dusty settled down on the bed and cleaned his Colts and the Spencer, then let his mother pack away his cleaning gear and fasten the bag. She fetched his bedroll with its tarp, suggans and blankets and rolled it neatly for him to take and strap to his saddlecantle.

After a meal Dusty took the gear out to the waiting horse and while Hondo fastened the bedroll on Dusty slid the carbine into the saddleboot his father had already fixed cavalry style to the left side of the saddle. Then he turned and kissed his mother and gripped his father's hand. He saw people looking, kinsfolk mostly and all good friends. They would be curious as to where he was headed but even if they asked, which wasn't likely, Hondo Fog would not tell them.

"Watch yourself down there boy," Hondo said as Dusty swung up into the saddle. "And if you have any trouble getting to see ole Bushrod Sheldon, or in getting him to listen to you, see Major Jubal Granger. He's an old friend of mine and he'll help you all he can. I reckon ole Jube will be just about ready to come on home again. And so will the other men."

"I'll do just that," Dusty agreed. "Reckon I'd better call in and see Uncle Tim, down to Brownsville. He's still the sheriff there?''

"Sure, he'll help you find the man.''

"I'l tell him you asked about him,'' Dusty remarked. "Any word for Aunt Martha while I'm there, maw?''

"Tell her I'm all right and that we'll try and visit them later in the year,'' Mrs. Fog replied. "You take care of yourself, son. Be careful.''

"I always am. Now don't you start in to sniffing, maw, or you'll likely start me going too.''

Mrs. Fog held down the tears, she managed a smile up at Dusty, then said: "You just take care.''

"Sure,'' Dusty agreed. "*Adios!*''

Hondo Fog put his arm round his wife's shoulders as they watched their son riding out of town towards the OD Connected. They stood there for a long time and watched him fade into the distance. Then they returned to the house again.

The following morning Dusty Fog stood on the porch of the ranch house and looked at Ole Devil Hardin and General Handiman.

"I've got your letter, but what's your message for Bush Sheldon?'' he asked.

Ole Devil grunted and held his hand out.

"You tell him to get back to the United States and stop his fooling around. There's only me'n Sam French left here and we're tired of handling these damned Yankees alone.''

CHAPTER THREE

Loncey Dalton Ysabel

DUSTY FOG'S BIG paint stallion picked an easy way along the winding trail through the thickly wooded Texas country. Dusty sat relaxed in the saddle, yet he was alert for every sound or movement. That sort of caution paid even on the better, more used trails. On a narrow sidetrack like this it was essential for there were bad whites and Mexicans roaming the wooded country and a man had been murdered for far less than a magnificent stallion, a good saddle and a brace of matched Colt revolvers.

With each loping stride of the big paint carrying him nearer to Brownsville Dustry grew more watchful and alert. So far nobody knew of his mission or his destination, of that he was sure. Handiman insisted that he hadn't told anyone why they were in the Rio Hondo. That was some consolation, for Dusty knew that he was in for a hard time even without the added hazard of the French knowing why he was going to see Bushrod Sheldon.

The man in Brownsville might, or might not be of help to him. Dusty was not even sure who the man would be for Handiman couldn't tell him. However the Cameron Country Sheriff was one of Dusty's numerous kin and might be able to help locate the man. If not Dusty meant to stay on only for two days, then strike south on his own.

The paint turned a sharp bend in the trail and came out into a clearing. Dusty halted the horse and looked round, alert and watchful for someone was camping here. A small fire was burning in the centre of the clearing, a coffeepot bubbling on it. A bedroll and warbag lay on the other side of the fire and at the far side of the clearing, looking at him, stood a magnificent white stallion not an inch smaller than Dusty's seventeen-hand paint. The horse was without bridle or saddle, they lay near the bedroll.

That was all, there was no sign of the owner of horse or outfit.

"Who'd you ride for in War, friend?"

The voice, soft, drawling and a musical tenor, seemed to float out of the air in a ventriloquial way. Dusty judged it to come from the left and went down off his horse on the "Injun side", left hand leaping across his body, the bone-handled Colt coming out cocked and ready. He stood very still, trying to locate the speaker. The woods lay silent all round the clearing, not even a bird stirring to help give him a clue. Apart from the two horses Dusty might have been alone here, but the voice came again to prove he was not.

"Asked a real sociable question, friend."

"Texas Light Cavalry," Dusty replied, twisting round slowly, almost sure the voice came from the far side of the clearing. "How about you?"

A short mocking laugh came from behind Dusty and the sound which might come from a cocking revolver. The small Texan spun round, dropping to one knee and firing in a flickering blur of movement at where the clicking sound came from. The bullet sent splinters flying as it sank into a thick tree and a voice which came from behind it said: "Don't shoot, I'm coming out."

A tall, Indian dark, black-dressed youngster stepped from behind the tree. He stopped and looked at the hole in the trunk then compared it with his own body and nodded. "Fair piece of offhand shooting a man'd say, friend."

Dusty looked the other over. He didn't look to be more than sixteen at the most but for all of that he was a dead cool hand. The bullet would have caught him in the body at heart level had he been stood in front of the tree instead of behind it.

"My own fault," the youngster went on. "Shouldn't have fooled about like that and then step on a rotten stick."

He came forward, giving Dust a better view of him. His black JB Stetson hat was hanging back by its storm-strap and his hair was curly, so black it shone almost blue in the light. His face looked handsome, young and innocent, almost babyish but those red-hazel coloured eyes were not young, they were old, watchful and hard. Like his hat and his hair all his clothing was black, from the silk bandana round his neck to his boots. Only the butt forward walnut grips of the old Dragoon Colt at his side and the ivory hilt of his bowie knife at his left relieved the blackness.

This youngster walked forward with the long-legged, free stride of a buck Apache. In his hands he held a second Colt Dragoon revolver, this one with a detachable canteen, carbine stock fitted on it.

"Howdy," he greeted as he halted in front of Dusty. "Smelled your dust a piece back and concluded to hide and see who you was before I showed."

"You expecting borrowing neighbours, friend?" Dusty inquired as he blew the smoke from the barrel of his Colt and holstered it. Such caution might mean the boy was on the run from the law, or just that he liked to pretend he was. Dusty was a shrewd judge of charcter and knew the boy was not the sort to be playing children's games.

"Man has to watch who comes up on him down here, happen he wants to grow up old and ornery," the boy replied. "Coffee's on the boil, light and take some."

"Thank you, friend," Dusty went to his paint and felt inside the bedroll, bringing out a tin cup. "One thing I learned in the army was always to keep my gun and coffee cup on hand all the time."

"I thought I'd seen you afore," the youngster took Dusty's cup and filled it with strong black coffee. "You're Cap'n Fog of the Texas Light. I saw you that time your pappy and Colonel Mosby told Quantrill just what they thought of him. You wouldn't have seen me, I warn't but a private and right at the back of the Mosby bunch." He paused and refilled his own cup. "The name is Loncey Dalton Ysabel."

"Better known as the Ysabel Kid?"

"To sheriffs, the border patrol and other kind of friends," the young man answered cheerfully. "You heard of me?"

"I've heard."

Dusty had heard plenty about a certain Indian dark young man called Loncey Dalton Ysabel, better known as the Ysabel kid. He'd also heard of the Kid's father, Sam Ysabel, as a prominent gentleman of the border smuggling bunch. Sam Ysabel was a wild Irish Kentuckian who'd come to Texas in the early days and rode as scout for Jim Bowie; riding scout was how he'd missed the Alamo. After the war with Mexico, Sam Ysabel pushed into the Comanche country and came back with a beautiful wife, daughter of Chief Long Walker and his French Creole squaw. Out of that dangerous mixture of bloods was born one child, a son who inherited the sighting eye of an eagle from the sure-shooting, rifle-toting Kentuckian stock. From the French Creole side he got a love of cold steel for a fighting weapon and the inborn ability to handle a knife. From his Comanche grandpappy he'd got his horse savvy, the ability to read sign where a buck Apache might falter. From all of them he'd gained a power of fight savvy and a willingness to match against anyone who tried to make him toe the line.

This was Loncey Dalton Ysabel. The Mexicans along the border said his name in whispers as an harbinger of death and destruction, yet there were many of them who called him friend. He was said to be good with his hand gun, a master at the noble art of knife fighting and beyond all par with a rifle. The rifle was not in evidence at the moment, or Dusty couldn't see it anywhere.

"Heard anything good?" the Kid asked.

"Some," Dusty grinned at the other youngster. The Rio Grande country did not come under Hondo Fog's jurisdiction as sheriff of Rio Hondo County so the Ysabel family had never come into conflict with the Fogs. In fact Dusty and his father were inclined to look on smuggling as the Ysabels did it as harmless and certainly not breaking any serious law.

"Your pappy along?"

"He's dead. Gunned down from behind by a pair of border rats called Giss and Krauss."

"I thought they worked for your pappy?" Dusty could read the pain and anger behind those soft drawled words and in the Comanche mean look in the red-hazel eyes.

"They did. Not regular, but when we couldn't get good men. Came to see us in our camp on the other side of the river, wanted us to sell some of our friends to the French. We wouldn't do that and they left the camp. Then while pappy was saddling up to ride and warn Don Ruis they shot him down from behind. That'll be Giss I reckon. He claims to be more than a fair hand with a rifle. Kraus tried to down me, bust my Hawken to hell and gone and lit out afore I could get to my ole Nigger hoss here." The Kid paused, his face still that inscrutable Indian mask. "I took after them and trailed them down towards the French at Neuva Rosita. Then when they got into the French camp they sent their renegade Mexicans after me. I lit out, a man can't handle that sort on their own ground. Come north to the line and crossed over. I've been hid out here for a couple of days. Happen I've given them the slip. I'll be headed back there again."

Dusty knew there was more to the quiet told story than just the bare facts as the Kid laid them down. He could picture the Indian dark boy trailing the men who murdered his father, cold, savage and more dangerous than any Comanche Dog Soldier. Then being hunted north by the Mexicans. Dusty pitied Giss and Kraus if the Ysabel Kid ever caught up with them.

"Sorry about your pappy."

"So'll Giss 'n' Kraus be when I meet up with them."

The Ysabel Kid had rested his carbine-stocked Dragoon on his saddle to pour out the coffee. He bent over the fire now to poke it up to a better blaze and was still bending forward when the big white stallion tossed back its head and snorted loud and hard.

At the same moment five dirty, ragged Mexicans burst out from the bushes at the far side of the clearing. They were a savage, hard looking bunch, each man holding a French muzzle loading carbine and all with a knife sheathed at their belts.

The sudden appearance might have taken the Kid by surprise, but his reactions were fast. He dived forward, hands reaching for the Dragoon gun leaning on his saddle and lit down rolling, earing back the hammer. He knew he would be too late to save himself, for although three of the Mexicans could not hit a barn from the inside, the other two were excellent shots and would not miss him.

This pair halted, lining their carbines on the rolling figure, the other three charging in closer but keeping out of the line of fire.

Dusty's tin cup fell, his hands crossing and the matched guns coming clear of leather and both roaring at the same instant. The two men who'd halted and lined their guns already both took lead. The man at the right dropped his rifle and his hands clawed up at his face as if trying to stop the blood which oozed from the hole between his eyes. The other man staggered as lead smashed into his arm, then he stumbled backwards with the carbine falling. Finally, he turned and ran for the shelter of the woods.

Dusty's shots had sounded before the cup hit the ground.

The big white stallion gave a scream of rage and raced after the wounded man. They disappeared from sight in the woods and after a moment a hideous cry shattered the air, mingled with the terrible screams of a fighting stallion and the sickening thuds as steel shod hooves tore into flesh.

The Kid bore a charmed life, aided by Dusty's shooting. The other three men fired at him on the run, which in itself was not conducive to good shooting, even when the nerves were not jarred by the lightning speed the small insignificant man drew and shot. Of the three carbine bullets one went into the fire sending sparks and flames erupting, the second kicked up dirt near Dusty and the third fanned just over the Kid's head as he came up and shot one. One of the trio rocked backwards, a small hole in his chest but what looked like half his back torn off where the .44 ball came out.

The last two Mexicans dropped their empty carbines and snatched out their long bladed, wicked looking knives. With these they were far more dangerous as they hurled straight at the Kid.

Dusty leapt to one side but he could not get a clear shot at the two men. He raised his right hand gun fast, eyes lining the V notch sight in the tip of the hammer with the foresight, then he fired once. The Ysabel Kid afterwards swore he felt the wind of that bullet passing him. The Mexican at his left was knocked back off his feet, hit in the right eye by Dusty's accurate and fast thrown shot.

The last man was in close. He brought the knife round and up in a driving rip which was aimed to lay the Kid open from belly to brisket. With a slower, less agile man this might even then have succeeded but the Ysabel Kid moved with all the inborn speed and fightsavvy of his Comanche ancestors. The butt of the carbine-stocked Dragoon gun came round parrying the knife which shattered its point against the tarnished silver plate inlaid in the woodwork. The Mexican, lunging forward with all his weight behind the blow was unable to stop himself and came right in on to the upswinging black clad knee as it drove for his groin. The Kid felt his knee ram home with all his power behind it and heard the man's agonised scream as he doubled over clutching the injured organs and stumbling past in a painwracked crouch.

Coming round fast the Ysabel Kid acted with savage, Comanche speed and lack of feeling. He gave the Mexican neither time to recover from his pain nor from his staggering, forward movement. The Dragoon's attached stock lifted and drove down with all the power of the Kid's lithe body behind it, sending the metal shod butt plate smashing into the Mexican's temple. It was a killing blow and from the way the Mexican's limp body flopped to the ground the Kid knew no further blow would be needed to end the affair.

Holding his Dragoon cocked and ready for instant use the Kid went around the bodies to make sure that no further trouble need be expected from that source. Then he stood looking down at Dusty's first victim and the fallen rifle which indicated the place the second stood before Colt lead reminded him of urgent business in some other place. They were some distance apart and yet the small man hit both of them, one fatally in that flickering half second from dropping his cup to planting the lead. The Kid was a fair hand with a revolver himself but he knew that here was a man who was the master of any he'd seen, up to and including one of his kin, the terror from Mill Creek, Bad Bill Longley.

"I called your shooting wrong," he said as he recalled the wind of the close-passing bullet. "it's more than fair and I never before saw a man who could use a gun with either hand the way you did."

Dusty did not regard his ambidextrous prowess with a gun as anything unusual. Yet it was and told a tale of a boy's determination to make up for his lack of inches some way. All his life Dusty had felt his small size had set him apart from the tall men of his clan. Even at school he'd been the smallest boy of the class although he'd never been bullied for it, he was too wild a scrapper for that. Yet in an attempt never to be noticed for his lack of inches Dusty forced himself to use either hand for every purpose from writing to shooting. His natural aptitude and perfect co-ordination between hand and brain made him a fine shot and gave him the extra flicker of speed so necessary to a man.

It was this ambidextrous skill and the tricks which Tommy Okasi taught him that enabled him to rise from private to Captain in command of a self-contained troop of Cavalry and to make older men obey him. The deadly and, apart from in the Orient, at that time unknown techniques of ju-jitsu and karate along with his speed helped him to handle himself in any kind of fight. Several larger men met with Dusty's knowledge of the Nippon fighting way called "the empty hand" learned that their rough house knowledge was of no use against him.

"Who are they?" Dusty indicated the still forms, although he could guess the answer even before it was given.

"Them borrowing neighbours you was talking about," the Kid replied. "The five *pelados* Giss and Kraus sent after me."

Dusty spoke fair Spanish and knew what *pelado* meant when spoken in the way the Kid just used the term. Literally the word meant one who removed the skin from a dead animal. Used as the Kid spoke it *pelado* meant the lowest form of thief on the border, the kind which would rob a dead body. These five looked as if they might have come into that category before their days of robbery and murder were brought to a not untimely end.

"Looked tolerable keen to get acquainted," Dusty remarked. Then he remembered the one the white stallion chased into the woods. "Your hoss took after one of them."

"Reckon he caught up with him," the Kid replied and whistled shrilly.

"Yeah," Dusty agreed as the white came out of the woods with blood on its legs. "I reckon he caught up with him."

Neither of the pair was worried about the killing of these five Mexicans. Both had been killing from necessity since their early teens and knew that in this case not only did they save their own lives but they finished five worthless careers with the possibility that they also prevented the five murdering others. That kind of Mexican bandit were without pity or mercy and would kill to rob without any scruples. The treacherous attack, if it had been successful would have caused the five Mexicans no conscience worries. It was better for the world in general and for the well-being of the two young Texans in particular that all five were dead.

"Let's move camp some," the Kid suggested. "This lot stink worse than a week dead polecat and they're crawling with seam squirrels. Must have come from downwind or that ole Nigger hoss of mine would have got on to them sooner. They handled it real nice. Man'd say it was lucky you was along here."

"They handled it nice."

"Sure, murder's their best play. They don't take to no shooting war, not with anybody who can handle a gun."

Dusty lifted the coffeepot from the fire and emptied it out. He looked around and the Kid indicated where he would find water. While Dusty took the pot along to wash it out and allow it to cool the black-dressed youngster rolled his warbag in his bedroll and slung it ready to be strapped to the saddle. He caught the big white stallion, checked it to make sure the Mexican hadn't managed to wound it, then saddled it and slipped on the bridle.

When Dusty returned the Kid lashed the coffeepot to the back of his bedroll then slid the Dragoon gun, still with the butt attached into his saddleboot. He gripped the saddlehorn and went into the saddle with a lithe, Indian like bound. Dusty caught his paint and mounted, looking at the Kid.

"You know this section better than I do, so lead on."

They rode off side by side. The Kid had put out the fire and now as the sound of their hooves faded off the silence came down once more, only broken by the soft buzzing of the flies which gathered round the five bodies.

Dusty watched the other young man as they rode along. There was an Indian caution in the way he lounged in his saddle and although he didn't seem to be taking any notice the Kid's eyes were never still and his ears tuned for any small sound which might serve as a warning to him.

Neither spoke but both were busy with their thoughts. Dusty thought over what he knew of this dark youngster who he'd saved from death. The Ysabel family were border smugglers and had been ever since the Unite States made taxable certain goods from both countries. To have lasted as long as they had needed skill, brains and local knowledge. It also meant they needed to be fighting men down to their wild Irish-Kentucky-Creole-Comanche toes and the Kid was all of that. It also meant he knew Mexico and the Mexican people, from the rich hacienderos down to the poorest, most ragged peons. That knowledge would be invaluable if he would ride with Dusty on this mission.

The Kid led on to such effect that he brought them to a pleasant clearing on the banks of a stream.

"Best night here," he said, looking round. "No place we

can get to worth going afore dark.''

They off-saddled and left the horses picketed apart for the two stallions were eyeing each other and snorting warningly. Then while the Kid lit a fire Dusty got his food out and started to make a meal.

With the food done they settled down on their bedrolls and started to clean their weapons. It was then that Dusty saw the two Dragoons were not a matched pair. The one from the holster was the older, Second Model, with the square-backed brass trigger-guard and the seven-and-a-half-inch barrel. The other was of the rounded trigger-guard, eight-inch-long barrel, and cut for the attachable carbine stock, which was known as the third model.

The detachable stock lay on the bedroll at the side of the Kid and was one of the rare canteen-containing kind which Dusty had read about but never seen before. So always eager to examine something new in the way of weapons he asked if he could look at the stock. The Kid's face was expressionless as he handed it over. Dusty saw this newer Dragoon was a finely engraved piece even as he turned the stock over and looked first at the canteen, then at the plate inlaid in the butt. The knife had only made a slight dent and he could read the lettering engraved in the silver.

''To Mason Haines from his friend Jethro Kliddoe.''

''Nice piece,'' Dusty remarked as he handed the stock back after examining it for a time. He wondered how it came to be in the hands of the Ysabel Kid, for that dark boy could not be Mason Haines, nor would a Mosby rider call Kliddoe friend.

''Sure,'' the Kid's voice was soft and gentle yet there was that Comanche mean look in his eyes again. ''One of these days I aim to head north and take it back to ole Yellerdawg Kliddoe.''

Dusty made no attempt to question this remarkable statement. Kliddoe had been the Union Army's equivalent of William Clarke Quantrill, a man who committed murder and plundered in the name of his flag and under the pretence of fighting for his cause. He would hardly be the sort of man a

Dixie boy would go out of his way to see at any time.

"What are you aiming to do now, Lon?" Dusty asked as he unrolled his gear to get fresh bullets for the guns.

"Waal, there were eight of them after me and Gis'll be just busting his pants to know how they got on. I'm headed back to tell him. Surely hate to see a friend unhappy and worried."

"Why not ride with me?" Dusty asked softly, watching the other's face, "I'm going south, too."

"Into Mexico?" the Kid inquired. "It's no place for a southern boy right now."

"I know. There are a few down there. That's why I'm going."

"To join ole Bushrod Sheldon?"

"To fetch him back home."

CHAPTER FOUR

A Dying Juarez Man

THERE wasn't a sound for the moment, the Kid's Indian dark face showing no expression as he looked at Dusty. He did not speak for some time, then remarked, "A man'd say you surely picked a real easy way to make a living."

Dusty shrugged, thinking the same thing himself. "Sure, but if General Bush don't come back we can't offer to send help to the Juaristas."

The Kid thought this over. He and his father supported the Juarez cause from both personal and business reasons. However with the Southerners fighting for Maximillian they steered clear of actual conflict with the French. The family smuggling business was feeling the troubles south of the border badly and until peaceful conditions returned again there was no point in a man trying to run contraband over the river. A man needed steady, reliable customers to run a successful smuggling organisation and there were enough forces of law and order arrayed against the smugglers without having to fight off French soldiers or Juarez irregulars who were from the south of Mexico, and did not know who a man was.

"I'll go along with you, Dusty. But I can't see Bushrod Sheldon coming back.

Dusty reached into his pocket and took out the letter handing it over. He knew that the message was private but some instinct told him that he could trust the Ysabel Kid and

37

that if he put his cards on the table this Indian-dark boy would be more than willing to help him.

The Kid read slowly, mouthing the words to himself and scowling at the more difficult pieces. However, even though much of the letter was in phrases he could not understand, he did know one thing. The Yankee Government wanted Bush-rod Sheldon back in the states and they wanted him really badly. There were concessions in that letter which made the Kid think and he knew that Bushrod Sheldon might even accept the terms. Word had it his men were tired both of the French and being so long away from home.

"I'll help you when you find Giss and Kraus then," Dusty promised. "I'll keep the rest of their men off you, if I can."

"That'll be all right with me. But we're going to have us one helluva time if the French find out that this letter is being sent. They'll be looking for us and if they find us they'll be on us foot, hoss and artillery."

"You'll be scaring me next."

The Ysabel Kid grinned at Dusty. He was getting to like and feel the magnetism of the small man. Somehow the Kid felt the same admiration for Dusty as he had for his father. They were much alike those two. Even though Dusty was small, soft-spoken and inconspicuous and his father was a big, wild black Irish Kentuckian. It was the air about them, an air that called for obedience and loyalty, the air of a born leader of men.

With the Ysabel Kid for an ally Dusty got down to the more serious work. He first of all prepared to load his guns. The Kid was stripping the caps from his carbine stocked Dragoon gun ready to load a couple of empty chambers. Removing the percussion caps from the others was a simple precaution for a chance knock could ignite them and fire the charge in the chamber, sending a ball out. Dusty opened a packet of Colt Combustible paper cartridges and extracted enough to reload the two revolvers. He was about to load them when he saw the Kid taking out some round moulded lead balls and a powder flask.

"Help yourself to these cartridges if you're out, Lon,"

Dusty remarked. "I've plenty of them to spare."

"Nope, thanks," the Kid juggled the balls in his hand. "You can keep them sort for me. Give me a soft lead round ball any time. It'll stop man or b'ar dead in his tracks first shot. Shaped bullets don't hit that hard."

Dusty laughed, watching the Kid feed powder into the chamber, then place the ball on it, pushing it home, turning the chamber under the hammer and forcing the ball home. Dusty ripped the protective foil from the cartridge and made a small hole in the cover, turned the chamber and rammed it home. They loaded the empty chamber in the same manner and then slipped the percussion caps on the nipples.

With their weapons loaded and ready for use Dusty got back to the business on hand.

"Where is Bushrod Sheldon?" he asked. "Last I heard he was down near Saltillo or Neuve Rosita."

"Neuve Rosita it is. There is a fair-sized garrison there, about five hundred men, French and the Sheldon boys. It's a hard country down there but I know it."

"Do you know the men who ride for Juarez down that way?"

"Sure, Don Ruis Almonte was one of the men Giss wanted to kill. He's a friend, we did plenty of business with him."

Dusty sat back and wondered if it was worth going to Brownsville and wasting time trying to locate the man Handiman told him would be there. With the Ysabel Kid riding along with him he might be able to do without whatever the other man might be able to give.

"Trouble is there's more than one bunch working that area," the Kid went on. "Some of them are all right, but there's others who aren't any better than those five we killed back there."

"We'll head down to Brownsville then," Dusty suggested, he explained about the man he was supposed to meet there.

The Kid was not too keen on going to Brownsville for Sheriff Tom Farron was one man he and his father steered well clear of when working on the border. However, such was the Kid's faith in Dusty Fog that he was willing to go not only to Brownsville, but to hell if necessary.

"Let's get some sleep first," he said.

They rolled on to their blankets and pulled the suggans over them, laying on top of the tarps, and were soon asleep under the stars, the two horses grazing and sleeping near by.

At the first light of morning Dusty and the Kid were awake and, after a wash and shave, and a meal, they saddled their horses and rode on their way towards the thriving town of Brownsville. They passed along quiet trails until finally a wider scar in the land was before them. The main Brownsville trail.

Riding alongside his new-found friend, the Ysabel Kid felt a new peace of mind, and a feeling of well-being stirred inside him. With the five men Dusty helped to kill, and the three he'd got himself in Mexico, there were no more Giss and Kraus men after him. Also he'd now a friend to ride along with him on his search for vengeance, a friend whose skill would be a help to him and one who would not spook or do something stupid in a tight corner.

He threw back his head and started to sing in a clear tenor:

"A Yankee come into West Texas,
     A sweet-talking hombre and sly,
     He fell in love with Rosemary Jo
     Then gave her the good-bye."

Dusty looked at the Kid, a smile flickering at his lips. There did not seem to be any end to the dark boy's talents. He sang like a bird and Dusty could guess that voice had often been raised as they rode the last few safe miles along some trail bringing a load of contraband.

"Now Rosemary Jo told her tough pappy,
     Who said, 'Now hombre, that's bad,
     In tears you're left my Rosemary Jo,
     I'll teach you you can't make her sad,'

> He whipped up his trusted old ten gauge,
>   At which—"

The song came to an abrupt end as the big white halted snorting and testing the wind as it fiddle-footed nervously. Instantly the Kid changed from a happy, singing man to a tense, hard-faced creature, no less savage than the big horse he rode. His right hand dropped and caressed the butt of his holstered Dragoon gun as his hazel eyes scoured the area. By his side, Dusty reached down and pulled out the Spencer ready for use, for he knew the horse was trained to give warning when men approached.

For a moment there was no sound, then from the thick bush up the trail a man stumbled. He staggered into the centre of the trail and fell to his knees, tried to get up and collapsed again.

It was then that the two different upbringings showed in Dusty Fog and the Ysabel Kid. Dusty, with all the instincts of the lawman, swung down from his horse to make an investigation. The Kid, however, stayed in his saddle and appeared to be contemplating a rapid escape.

Seeing Dusty going towards the man, the Kid swung down from his white and, with his old Dragoon in his hand, went forward. Then he scowled. The man wore a light blue, silver filigreed uniform, and his head was bare. The Kid knew that uniform, it was one worn by a crack regiment which rode for Juarez. The young Mexican was forcing himself up on to one hand while the other tried to pull loose the Colt from his holster. His handsome face was lined with agony and his eyes glazed over. It didn't need a doctor to look at the blood-running hole in the man's back to know he wasn't long for this world.

"Lie still, señor," the Kid's fluent Spanish call stopped the move. "We are friends. Who did this, are they near?"

The young Mexican collapsed again and Dusty rested his carbine on the ridge at the side of the trail, then bent over him. Gently he turned the wounded man over and looked down. The bullet which struck him in the back had come right through, and there was nothing anyone could do for the man. In fact, for a moment Dusty and the Kid thought he was dead for he laid so still, hardly even breathing. Then his eyes came open and he looked up at the two men bent over him.

"Ambush—French!" he gasped out in halting Spanish, not recognising them but talking with the last of his breath. "Guns for Juarez. Tell—Brownsville—tell—get—guns—Monterrey."

The blood bubbled up from out of his mouth and his body. With a final convulsive quiver, the slender, handsome young man went limp. In his last breath he'd delivered them a message in the belief they were his friends.

"He's cashed," the Kid remarked, then made what to him was a natural suggestion: "Let's ride!"

"Not yet," Dusty replied. "I'll search him, then we'll lay him on the side of the trail and send a buggy out to collect him."

"Won't do no good searching him. The Juarists don't go a lot on writing when they send messages."

Dusty was already checking the young Mexican's pockets and the Kid looked his satisfaction at having his statement verified. He watched the way Dusty worked and got an uneasy suspicion he'd seen this kind of acting and thinking before. The suspicion was confirmed at Dusty's next question.

"Who do you reckon he is, Lon? And where did he come from?"

"He's a member of the 18th Rancheros, they're light cavalry, like your bunch. Most part formed of Creoles, younger sons of the hildagos and such."

"Do you know him?"

"Nope. There's a couple of folk in Mexico I don't know."

"Where did he come from just now?" Dusty eyed his friend grimly. "And don't tell me from that bus. I've seen that."

"You talk like a lawman," the Kid growled back. "Act like one, too."

"And you talk like a dead mean ole smuggler," Dusty shot back. "Hear tell you can read sign a mite."

"A mite," the Kid was cautious now. "What you thinking of doing?"

"Getting a full story ready for when we get to Brownsville. I want to tell the sheriff—"

"Tell the sheriff?" the kid groaned. "You mean go into Brownsville, ride up to ole Tim Farron's office and go in, without being took at gunpoint?"

"Sure, that's the way I usually do it."

"Well, it ain't my way," the Kid objected, for he could see all too clearly what would happen if he rode merrily up to the County Sheriff's office and announced he'd found him a dead body. Tim Farron was not the best friend the Ysabel family had. He was a lawman and a good one but to the Kid's mind was over-zealous in his duties regarding the prevention of smuggling. There were lawmen who took smuggling to be a pleasant and legal business which supplied them with cheap goods and an extra amount of wealth. There were others who said that smuggling was against the law and tried, without success, to stop it. Tim Farron was one of the latter.

"You scared?"

"Sure, I don't like going near jails. Pappy always tole me lookings might be catchings. So I don't look."

"Tell you, then, you backtrack him and see where he'd come from. I'll see the sheriff." Dusty was enjoying the Ysabel Kid's worried look at the thought of going voluntarily to see a sheriff so did not mention that Tim Farron was his uncle.

"All right, I'll do it. My pappy warned there'd be days like this."

They lifted the body clear of the trail and laid it under a bush. The Kid took an old bandana from his pocket to hang on the branch of a tree and leave it swaying in the breeze. That would scare off any buzzard or even the wild pigs which infested the bush and which might get at the body while they were going to fetch the sheriff.

Then he turned and started to walk towards the woods.

Dusty called, "Here Lon, take this with you, it'll be more use than that old hand cannon."

The Ysabel Kid turned and caught the Spencer Dusty tossed to him, flipped open the lever and jacked a bullet into the chamber, then went into the bush. He found the stumbling marks left by the young Mexican with no trouble at all and followed them with no great difficulty. He hefted the carbine, feeling its agreeable weight in his hands and grinning a little as he thought of the small soft-spoken young man who'd taken charge of him so completely. It would be lonely down along the Rio Grande now old Sam Ysabel was gone. A man could not run the smuggling game on his own either. Yet there was little other than that the Kid thought himself qualified to do. He could handle cattle, but his work along that line was always done at night and mostly with little of the care a legal ranch owner insisted on when handling stock.

There was little of legal use he could put his hand to, for there was no call to know the winding smuggler trails along the big river, not as an honest and hard-working young citizen. He could read sign and was a fair hand at breaking a bad horse, but they were purely part-time occupations.

Anyhow, the Kid mused, as he followed the tracks, there was no certainty that they would come out of this business alive, and the chances were greatly against their so doing. If they did there would be time for a man to make up his mind to go or stay.

The sign was so plain that any half-bright Comanche boy could follow it, happen he had both his eyes going and it wasn't too dark a night. The young Mexican had shown guts to come this far. He'd crawled some of it and stumbled the rest, leaving some blood behind to mark his way, even if there wasn't a crushed growth and broken twigs for a man to follow.

Then the Kid found a blood-stained bandana laying on the tracks and after that there was no blood. This was simply explained: the young Mexican stopped the flow of blood with that bandana until he reached this spot. Likely he'd been too weak to hold on to it any more.

From that point the sign was not so plain, not that the Kid experienced any difficulty in following it. All his young life he'd been reading sign and could have followed far less evidence than this wounded man left. The tracks led on to be crossed twice by other human tracks, a big, burly man had searched down here since the Mexican passed. A man who searched the bushes but could not read sign for he'd crossed the Mexican's line twice. The Kid was alert, ready to take action at the slightest indication he was being watched. A man who'd shoot another in the back was not the sort one took chances with.

The sign led on to the bottom of a steep, red-soiled cliff face. Here by some quirk of nature the soil was left bare and the earth told the story to eyes which were long used to reading the messages of the ground. One patch was disturbed by someone coming down in a half-roll, half-slide. That would have been the young Mexican. He'd been lucky to get down without serious injury, and he'd taken cover in the bushes as the Kid already knew. Then he'd moved off again along the line the Kid followed here.

There were another set of footprints in the red soil. Both the toes pointed upwards but the Kid knew from their shape and cut that one set was made as a man came down, lowered by a rope and walking. That would be the only way a man could get down or up the slope on his two feet. A rope tied to some tree at the top, then come down it hand over hand, feet braced against the soil, digging in and leaving a real clear imprint.

The boots were high-heeled, though the soles looked blunter than the usual style a cowhand wore. They were boots meant for riding, to cling to the stirrup and give a brace to the legs, not for walking in. He would know that sign anywhere and if he ever saw it again he would be able to identify it without difficulty.

The Kid surveyed the slope but knew that without a rope he would have a lot of trouble to get up there. Even if he got up there he would not be able to do a thing, for the man who'd come down here was on a horse and would likely be well back to the Rio Grande by now. The young Mexican said something about an ambush by the French, which meant they'd got him and they'd be French soldiers after him. The Kid knew that any French soldier who was above the line would hardly wait round. He'd do his work and light out fast.

So the Ysabel Kid returned in the way he'd just come, striding along at a good speed. However, he was alert and something caught his eye on the way back. It lay in the bushes, a small saddlebag, half hidden from view even from this side. From the way he'd come the Kid would be unable to see it. He'd been concentrating on the tracks coming and giving no attention to any side issues.

The saddlebag was made of good quality leather and bore the crest of the 18th Rancheros. It was only fastened with a buckle, but the Kid did not open it; instead he slung it over his shoulder and returned to the Brownsville trail where Dusty was waiting.

"Where did he come from?" Dusty asked.

"Back there in the bush. Must have been bad hit some ways back. Tracks ended for me at a slope. I couldn't climb. He'd come down it, likely got hit at the top. Crawled into the bushes and hid out. Another man came down the slope. Used a rope to get down. Might mean there were more of them at the top. He came down and made a search, but couldn't read sign any. Crossed the Mexican's line twice and never saw it."

"Could have been French soldiers after him," Dusty remarked. "That means they'll have lit out for the border real fast. They wouldn't want to be taken in uniform on United States soil."

"Killed a man in cold blood, but they wouldn't know he'd been found. Why'd they light out? I allow they'd come along the Brownsville trail here and see if they could find him."

"Not if they're in uniform," Dusty objected.

"Uniform or not, they could hang just as high—"

"That's not it, Lon. It's international law. We don't recognise the Maximillian Government in Mexico and to us the French and Mexicans are fighting. So if we catch any of their nationals wearing uniform we have to intern, hold them until peace is declared or other arrangements is made.''

"Say, I found this saddlebag," he said, showing it to Dusty. "Reckon we can see what is in it?''

"Why sure," Dusty agreed, taking the bag and opening the flap.

"Wowee!" the Kid whooped. "Man, I never saw so much money in one lump in all my wicked and young life.''

Dusty thumbed through the stack of notes. They were all hundred-dollar bills and formed a fair amount.

"What are we going to do with it?" the Kid asked, then groaned. "Oh, no! Dusty, you ain't going to turn all that money over to Tim Farron?''

"Sure we are," Dusty replied. "What did you think of doing with it?''

"Know a hollow tree where we could hide it until we come back from Mexico," the Kid suggested. "Then we could buy us new clothes, a couple of them Henry repeaters and I'd take you to see a few places along the bord—''

Dusty shook his head, watching with some amusement the play of emotion on the Ysabel Kid's face as he realised that Dusty was determined to give the money over to the law.

"Wouldn't miss a couple of them," he went on.

"Likely, but we'll hand it in. Wait a minute, what was he saying, the Mexican, just before he died?''

"Something about guns for Juarez, take them to Monterrey," the Kid growled, as he eyed the saddlebag. "All right, but when you die and go wherever you're going and they ask you what you ever did bad in your life, you tell them you ruined a poor lil ole quarter Comanche boy for good.''

"How'd you mean?''

"Why coming here, taking me to see the sheriff and toting in all that money and not taking none of it for our trouble. I tell you Dusty, my kin'll stop talking to me, sure as I'm born.''

CHAPTER FIVE

A Plug Hat from New Haven

THE town of Brownsville, Texas, was large and prosperous. From the port in the war ranged Confederate blockade runners. Now trade poured in here both from Mexico and from over the Atlantic. It was a town of contrasts, seamen of many nationalities thronged the streets and the dock area while further back could be found farmers, cattlemen and others who made their living from the lush and fertile lands of Cameron county.

Cowhands were no novelty here and none noticed the two men who rode in that early afternoon. This suited Dusty Fog and the Ysabel Kid, particularly the latter for he was unused to city life and disliked being crowded in by people. He also disliked seeing uniformed city marshals watching him.

"You still aiming to go and see the sheriff?" he asked.

"Why sure."

"Then let's pull in here and have a meal at the saloon. I hear ole Tim Farron don't feed his prisoners too good and he'll surely jail us as material witnesses when we tell him."

Dusty grinned cheerfully; the Kid was worried that his reputation as a smuggler remained untarnished by a visit of his own free will to a sheriff. Dusty was just as determined that they do the right thing and report the murder to the county authorities so an investigation and report could be made. However he felt hungry and did not want to drop in on his Uncle Tim unexpectedly. He turned his horse towards the saloon, hearing the Kid's sigh of relief at this reprieve.

The Eagle saloon was not busy as they pushed through the batwings, only a party of five or so cavalry troopers drinking at the bar and from the look of them well on the way to being carried out. They were talking loud and boastfully and one huge, red faced soldier looked to be their ringleader. Dusty frowned. He was still military enough to want to take the soldiers and bounce them clear out of the saloon right straight to the stockade where they would learn that drunkenness didn't pay.

The two young Texans stood at the door for a moment watching the troopers, then a man came into the bar from the rear door which led to the living quarters.

"Now there's a man dressed for trouble if I ever saw one," the Kid remarked.

The man was dressed for trouble anywhere west of the Big Muddy, in a style that was more correct for the eastern city, not for the wild frontier country of Texas. A pearl-grey plug hat sat back on his head, the face was reddened by the sun, but was impressive with its stylish moustache and neatly trimmed goatee beard. He wore an expensive and well cut black Prince Albert jacket, white shirt and large polka dotted bow-tie, tight legged grey trousers, spats and boots. The main wonder of the stylish gent's attire was that he wore no gun nor could Dusty's trained eyes locate any sign of a hidden weapon.

The soldiers at the bar nudged each other as they saw the man come into the room. The biggest of them moved from his place at the bar and grinned at the others.

"What we got here, boys?" he asked. "It looks like some deck's gone shy a joker, don't it?"

The others all howled with laughter at this and one of them whooped, "Listen to ole Cooney. He's a real rip, ain't he?"

The big dude stopped, his moustache bristling with rage. "He looks more like a drunken bum and a disgrace to his uniform to me."

Cooney stiffened and pushed his big face forward. "Is that right, Percy?" he snarled out. "Why you fancy—"

The dude might look fancy but he moved fast and with a strength and skill that showed he could handle himself. His right fist shot out from the shoulder in a punch which carried all his weight behind it. It was the sort of punch that ended a fight as soon as it started. Of its strength and power Cooney could have given testimony and did after he recovered.

Cooney's head rocked back under the impact of the punch, his feet shot out as they tried wildly to hold the floor, then he crashed down on to his back. The other soldiers stared down in amazement, expecting Cooney to bound up and tear the dude limb from limb. Then it dawned on their drink-slowed minds that Cooney was not going to get up for some time.

One of the troopers grabbed for his gun, hand twisting round to make the fast done cavalry draw. His gun was clearing out when the fast dude's cane rattled down on his wrist making him howl and drop his weapon. The others moved from the bar, fists clenched.

"Attention!"

The Ysabel Kid almost leapt out of the door as Dusty roared out that one word. His friends's voice was changed from that easy soft spoken drawl to a tone the Kid and the soldiers knew. It was the tone of a savage disciplinarian, an officer who meant to be obeyed.

Those soldiers did not doubt the authenticity of that voice even though they could not see any officer. It was the sort of voice that set a rigid iron bar down even the most drunken and whisky-soaked spine. They waited for the next order to come, thinking one of their officers was outside.

With his back to them Dusty gave his next order, "Pick up that drunken gold-brick then march out. Move!"

The door of the saloon opened and a big, hard-looking sergeant stood there. "Well, if it ain't Mr. Cooney's friends," he said sarcastically eyeing the men. "And what happened to Mr. Cooney?"

"This dude put him down," a trooper answered.

"Then he's a gentleman to be commended. Cap'n Adams'll be real pleased to hear how you've been drinking when you were on stores detail. Get hold of him and march back to the barracks."

The soldiers left carrying Cooney but the sergeant stayed inside looking round. He glanced at the two young Texans then at the dude, then shaking his head he walked out again.

The dude came across the room, holding his hand out and smiling broadly. "An excellent ruse if I may say so, sir," he said as he gripped Dusty's hand. "That could have developed into a nasty situation. Egad, I almost wish I'd been wearing a gun."

"War's over friend. They hang a man for shooting blue bellies now," the Kid replied.

"I suppose so. May I offer you liquid refreshment?"

"Not unless it's a cold beer," Dusty answered. "We only came in here for a meal."

"Then you must be my guests. Take a seat gentlemen," he turned and yelled across the room, "Charles, a libation. My guests require cold beer and I will take my usual. Give my compliments to the chef. I have two guests and will require a fitting repast. Preferably some of his excellent son-of-a-bitch stew. If that meets with your approval, gentlemen?"

"Why sure," Dusty agreed as he and the Kid took their seats at a table.

The big man sat down with a flourish, produced his cigar case and offered it across the table, but the Texans refused, preferring to roll their own smokes with paper and Bull Durham. After lighting the smokes the big man broke his match and dropped it into the ash-tray.

"May I introduce myself, gentlemen. I am Thomas Emery Alden, traveller, salesman, agent-extraordinary for the Winchester Repeating Firearms Company of New Haven. Whom do I have the pleasure of addressing?"

The name meant nothing to Dusty or the Kid as yet for Winchester were not as yet bringing out weapons in their own name, still calling their product the Henry rifle. Dusty thought the man was a salesman for one of the numerous crackpot little companies which were trying to make a successful repeating rifle that was capable of doing its work and cheap enough to be practical.

After the introductions were over the talk turned to more normal channels, the cattle business or lack of it, the War and the trouble below the border. On each subject Alden talked with some knowledge. He was an accomplished talker and a man with some education, that was plain. However, much to Dusty's surprise Alden neither tried to sell or interest them in his company's product.

The food was good and after the meal they sat back and talked some more. They were still talking when three men wearing Mexican dress came in. Alden looked the men over as they went to the bar and spoke softly to the bartender who pointed to the table where Dusty sat with the Kid and Alden.

The three Mexicans came across the room. They were tall men and more heavily built than the usual run of vaquero. Each carried a revolver in an open topped holster but none wore a knife.

"Señor Alden?" the tallest of the trio asked.

"I am sir," Alden spoke good Spanish. "What can I do for you?"

"May I speak with you on a matter of some importance and of a confidential nature?"

"You may," Alden pushed back his chair, nodded to Dusty and the Kid. "I hope you'll excuse me. I've some business to attend to with these gentlemen."

It was then Dusty saw the butts of the Mexicans' guns. He noticed the Ysabel Kid was watching the Mexicans and frowning, so wondered what was worrying his young friend.

The guns carried by the three Mexicans took his attention again, particularly the butts. They were not the smooth, hand-fitting curve of the Colt, the finest pointing grip ever made for a hand-gun. These were black, round and more straight. Always interested in weapons Dusty thought of how they would be awkward guns to line on a draw. Then he remembered.

It was back in the War, he'd been sent with his troop to collect a consignment of foreign firearms smuggled through the Yankee blockade. Amongst those arms were handguns like these. He thought back, trying to remember more about the guns. They'd been called Lefauchex revolvers and only moderately popular with the men who were issued with them. Lefauchex was a French firm.

It was then the Kid spoke. He'd been watching the three Mexicans who were now seated at another table with Alden and eating a meal as they talked with them. The Ysabel Kid frowned and catching Dusty's eye jerked his head towards the door. Dusty pushed his chair back and got to his feet, then waved a cheery good-bye to Alden and walked out. The Kid followed him out and on the sidewalk they looked at three horses which were fastened to the hitching rail.

"Something wrong, amigo?" the Kid asked.

"Something. Those three in there are wearing French guns."

"Are they?" The Kid didn't look too surprised at this. "A whole lot of the Juarez men do. They take them the same way we took arms in the war. You never rode for the 1st New York Volunteers and I surely ain't a friend of ole Yellerdawg Kliddoe."

Dusty took the point. The Juarez men, like the rebels, went in for replacing their arms with battlefield captures. However there was more to it than that. Dusty was sure the men were not what they seemed.

"They were new issued guns from the look of them. I never saw a Mexican who'd take good care of his gun."

"Wouldn't say that, Dusty. But you're right when you say there's something bad wrong. Those three *hombres* talk real good Spanish, but its not Mexican Spanish they're talking. You wouldn't know that, but I do.

"They're not talking it right?"

"Sure they talk it right, but not like they'd learned it in Mexico."

Dusty went to the horses and looked them over. They were three big, strong looking bays with military saddles. In the saddleboots were short, singleshot Charlesville carbines. Then he lifted one of the stirrup irons. It was coated with red mud.

Stepping back on to the porch Dusty glanced through the window. "Lon look at those three."

The Kid looked through the window but his face showed that he saw nothing more than the three men eating with Alden. "What about them?"

"They're holding their knives in the right hand."

"So?"

"We use the left hand for our knives, so do the Mexicans. Folks in Europe use their right."

"Do tell," the Kid still could not follow Dusty's line of reasoning.

"Sure, those three aren't Mexicans, they're French. Remember that Mexican we found out there on the trail?"

"Why sure. You reckon they're the three who dropped him?"

"Could be. Say! Alden said he was a salesman for some company and the Mexican was mumbling something about guns for Juarez." Dusty paused then looked up and down the street. "When we go in there again get set, I'm going to try something."

The Kid studied his young friend for a moment. He did not know what Dusty had in mind but he'd an idea that things were going to happen fast and furious in the near future. He glanced to make sure his horse was loose and ready to make a fast departure from town. Tim Farron wasn't going to be any too pleased to see Sam Ysabel's son any time, and he was going to like the Ysabel Kid even less after Dusty was through.

Dusty and the Kid entered the saloon again, the three men at the table were still talking to Alden and took no notice. Dusty glanced at the Kid to make sure he was set ready for action. Then Dusty opened his mouth and bellowed out:

"Aux armes! Aux armes! Juaristas."

The three men came to their feet, swinging round with angry, startled words bursting from their lips. Alden looked up, his face showing surprise. Not at the sudden shout or the way the three men leapt up, that was normal. The men shaken by the sudden shout were talking in French.

"*Sacre diable!*" the biggest snapped as he realized what he'd done. His hands dropped towards his gun as the other two also made their move.

Alden's chair went over backwards as the big man rolled back, crashing to the floor and twisting in an attempt to avoid the bullet he knew would be coming his way:

Ahead of all the others Dusty's matched guns were out, he threw a shot into the man who was trying to draw on Alden. The bullet smashed into the man's arm, knocking him backwards. The other two stood fast, they were covered by the Ysabel Kid's old Dragoon Colt.

The bardog who'd disappeared under the bar at the first sign of trouble came up again. He was debating what action to take when the small young man made up his mind for him by sending him for the sheriff.

The Kid stared his unbelief at Dusty, wondering what he was letting himself in for. He could see the inhospitable cell doors slamming on to him even now.

Dusty looked across the room at Alden who got to his feet and rubbed his hips. "Egad, that's the second time you've saved me from a serious and perilous position, Dusty. These men are French.

"Why sure," Dusty agreed, then went on in French. "Who are you?"

"Major Harmon, Blue Hussars," the wounded men gritted through his teeth.

"Attend to the Major," Dusty ordered the other two. "Lon, get their guns."

The Ysabel Kid did as he was ordered, moving behind the men and substituting his knife for the gun as he went in close. He removed the guns and then went back to stand by his friend.

The sheriff and the town marshal both arrived at once. Tim Farron stopped and looked over the scene, his eyes were distinctly unfriendly as he looked the Kid over or that was the impression Loney Dalton Ysabel got.

"All right, what happened here?" he asked.

The Kid looked at Dusty and groaned inwardly. They

would soon be in jail and he didn't like the idea of being cooped up in a cell. It was Dusty who answered:

"Howdy Uncle Tim. These three killed a Mexican. His body is on the edge of the Brownsville trail."

Farron gave his illustrious young nephew a warm smile. "Howdy, Dusty. You sure about it?"

"Sure enough," Dusty replied and told of the finding of the body. "Lon here cut their sign and followed it to the slope. You'll find the same soil as the slope on one of the stirrup irons."

The Ysabel Kid had been trying to efface himself from sight and felt very uneasy as Tim Farron turned round. A big hand reached out to him and Farron grinned warmly. "Howdy, boy. How's your pappy?"

The Ysabel Kid was still dazed after Tim Farron left with his three prisoners for he could not believe that not only was he still free but that Tim Farron had actually shaken hands with him and been friendly. Dusty went out of the saloon with his uncle and told something of his reason for being down this way. Farron could not even offer to help locate the man from Washington for the town was filled with a floating population.

Alden and the Kid were seated together at a table in the saloon when Dusty returned. The big man looked worried and there was something like relief in his eyes as Dusty came up.

"This puts me on the horns of a dilemma." Alden remarked. "As I was just telling the Kid here. Look, would you care to come along the street with me?"

"Why sure, we've got nothing more to do for a spell."

The three men left the saloon and went along to a small wooden building. Alden unlocked the door and waited for the two Texans to leave their horses, then led the way in.

There was only one room, small, square and windowless. Alden lit a lamp and the other two found themselves looking at boxes which crowded the place out almost to where they stood. Some of the wooden boxes were small and square, the others long and oblong in shape. All bore the stencilled words. "Winchester Repeating Firearms Company, New Haven."

Alden went to the nearest of the long boxes and took out a rifle, coming back to the others and asking, "What do you think of this?"

"A Henry rifle," the Kid breathed out the words almost reverently. "Man, with one of these you can load on Monday, shoot Yankees all week and still have lead to go coon hunting on Sunday."

Dusty did not show the same enthusiasm for he'd handled several Henry rifles. "They're not bad, nigh as good a repeater as you could buy these days. But I found the extractor a mite weak and the magazine slot got clogged up with dirt easily, gets dented and jammed real easy, too."

"A discerning eye, I see," Alden replied. "They were structural defects in the earlier Henry rifles which we've almost eradicated in these. They make a good weapon." Alden took the rifle to the box and replaced it, taking out another. "These are far better."

The second rifle looked much like the Henry at first glance, but a second showed the difference. There was a wooden foregrip along part of the magazine and a slot in the side of the frame that was not present with a Henry rifle of the old pattern. All in all the new rifle looked much stronger and reliable.

There was pride in Alden's voice as he showed off the rifle and explained its points to his interested audience.

"You will notice that you load the magazine through this slot in the frame here. That allows us to strengthen the magazine tube. The magazine holds sixteen shots and a further one in the breech. Another useful innovation is that even when the gun has a full magazine single shots can be loaded into the breech allowing one to use it as a single shot but also to have sixteen ready loaded charges when needed."

Dusty nodded in approval as he hefted the rifle. It felt good in his hands but was still, in his opinion, too long and heavy for an effective saddle-weapon. The Ysabel Kid on the other hand held no such worries. There was eagerness in the way he took the rifle and tossed it on his shoulder, left eye closing and right eye as he focused along the barrel.

"So this is the new Henry?" he asked as he reluctantly handed the rifle back to Alden.

"It is," Alden agreed.

The Winchester Repeating Firearms Company had not yet renamed the rifle which was later to become famous as the "old yellow boy", the Model 66 and the first of their long line of lever action rifles bearing the company name. At the moment it was still known as the new, improved Henry.

It was a rifle that the Kid would have given his soul for. A repeater which really worked and which carried seventeen shots yet was light and compact enough for normal use. On the banks of the Rio Grande a man could use such a weapon to great advantage. More than any other weapon he'd ever seen the Kid wanted to own one of those new Henry rifles.

"How much would a man have to pay for one of those new Henry rifles?" he asked, never taking his eyes from the gun which Alden still held.

"They aren't for sale as yet. But I have twelve of them for Benito Juarez and his staff." Alden watched the disappointment flickering on the Kid's face. "I've been here for a month now waiting for a messenger from Juarez, but it appears he is dead and also that I must take the rifles to Monterrey if I want to sell them. Now if I could find a couple of smart young men who knew Mexico and would act as my guides there I would be willing to present them with one of these new model Henry rifles, a hundred dollars each and five hundred of the best Tyler B. Henry forty-four rimfire bullets."

The Kid looked at Dusty. There was pleading in the red hazel eyes and Dusty knew that more than anything in the world his young friend wanted that rifle. It was a hard decision to make. If they went with Alden there would be no chance of waiting for General Handiman's man, but those rifles would make Juarez more than pleased to see them. With that many repeaters and with Bushrod Sheldon's men out of the way Juarez would be able to strike the French hard and drive them from his country.

"We'll take on, Tom," he said, watching the delight on the Kid's face. "If you remember one thing. We'll only be able to get you to the town of Monterrey. If we get there and you sell the guns that is the end of our deal. We've some business of our own in Mexico and can't take time out to come back north with you. Is that all right?"

"Most certainly. Once we've sold the rifles I will make my own way back. No doubt Juarez will give me an escort with the money."

The Ysabel Kid laughed. He took the rifle and caressed it, hefting it with all the pleasure of a child with a new toy. "You watch that escort, Tom," he warned. "Was I you I'd pay them off as soon as you can and try to make it alone."

"I'll take your word for it. Now, as to the transporting of the rifles. I have wagons—"

"Wagons?" the Kid put in, taking his eyes off his new rifle for a moment. "You can't get through with wagons. The French know about these arms and they'll be out looking for them. We're going to have to take them overland."

"Overland?" Alden stared at the Kid. "There are a thousand stand of arms here and fifty thousand rounds of ammunition. How can we move that much overland?"

"Happen we're lucky we can do it. I'll be riding out of here and see if I can find a man. He should be within a day of here. I'll be back in two."

Alden asked no questions and Dusty went to the door with the Kid. He watched the young man slide the Winchester into his saddleboot and stuff the bullets Alden gave him into his bedroll.

"What's amusing you, Lon?" Dusty asked.

"Plenty. A sheriff shakes my hand and acts like he's pleased to meet me and I've got me a new repeating rifle."

CHAPTER SIX

Canebrake Country

"TOM, this here's Mike Conway."

It was two days after the meeting with Alden and the Ysabel Kid returned to Brownsville bringing a big, bearded and cheerful looking Irishman. They were at the small wooden store again.

"Mike," Alden greeted. "Pleased to meet you. Now how about these arms, Lon?"

"We've got to get them through, Mike," the Kid explained. "And we can't use wagons. The French will be patrolling the wagon trails, so there ain't but one way we can do it."

"You mean on mules?" Conway asked. "Lon, you're a darling boy to think of your poor ole Uncle Mike."

"There are a thousand rifles and fifty thousand round of ammunition," Alden pointed out. "That will take a lot of mules."

"Sure and I've got a lot. We'll break all the rifles out and wrap 'em up in tarps and we've carried boxes the size of the others many the time," Conway replied.

Dusty looked the Kid up and down, wondering if the young man could bring this off. He could see the impossibility of taking the wagons into Mexico and that the only possible way of getting the arms through would be on mules. He'd run mule trains of arms himself, but never in numbers like this.

Conway examined the new model Henry rifles and grunted in satisfaction at them. He could see no great difficulty in getting the rifles through on mules and after a short discussion on money agreed to go along.

"One thing I don't like is the French knowing not only about the shipment but who you were, Tom. That means they're on to you. They'll be watching for you and we don't want that. So this is what I reckon we should do," Dusty said.

The others listened intently for they knew who Dusty Fog was and they were willing to put themselves under his care.

So the following morning Dusty, the Kid, Alden and two of Conway's men headed for a ford of the Rio Grande above the town of Brownsville. Conway's men sat on the driving seats of Tom Alden's two wagons and the other three rode ahead. Dusty wanted the French to be looking for two wagons and not for mules. His guesswork was proved correct as they turned a corner in the trail and approached the ford. At the nearer side a couple of Sibley tents were erected and a young Lieutenant with four troopers were standing outside them. On the other side were several French soldiers commanded by a hard faced young Captain.

The young Lieutenant stepped forward as the wagon approached and held up his hand. "Are you Mr. Alden?" he asked.

"I am sir. May I help you in any way?"

"Only by turning back, sir. The French Government has made representations to Washington on the subject of your mission. My orders are to prevent you from crossing the border here."

"What!" Alden boomed back, his face reddening even deeper.

"Those are my orders, sir. You will have to turn back. Washington does not want international complications at the moment."

"Wait, please," the voice came from the other side of the ford. "I will come across if I may."

The French Captain rode across the river and halted,

saluting the Lieutenant casually and introducing himself. "Are these the men?"

"These are the gentlemen I was asked to turn back if that is what you mean."

"Then you will arrest them?" and when the Lieutenant shook his head, "I will call my men across and do it then."

"There will be no arrest," the young Lieutenant turned his gaze to the other Americans as he spoke. "These gentlemen are citizens of the United States I may remind you. My orders are to make sure that they do not cross the ford and I will remain *here* to make sure they do not. I hope that is understood by all concerned?"

Dusty caught the emphasis on the word "here" and nodded in agreement. He for one clearly understood what was meant.

Alden did not appear to have caught the sign, for his face went deeper red and he snapped, "This is intolerable. I will return to Brownsville and telegraph my company. We are not without friends in Congress as you'll soon find out."

"*Monsieur*," the Frenchman's face grew dark and angry. "My orders from Vera Cruz are to arrest this man. May I fetch my men over and do so?"

"You may not," the Lieutenant snapped back. "These gentlemen are United States citizens and on American soil. If you bring armed men across the river I will be compelled to regard it as a breach of international law and an act of open war. If Mr. Alden should cross into Mexico then you may do what you like."

Alden growled an angry curse and ordered his men to turn their horses back in the direction they'd come. When they were out of sight of the ford he threw back his head and roared with laughter.

"That young officer was smart," he said. "He'll be staying at that ford and not patrolling. It all falls on you now, Lon. Do you know a way across the river?"

"Why sure," the Kid replied. "See this *bosque* country here?" He indicated the woods on either side of the trail. "Upstream from here runs the canebrakes, behind the trees.

We're going through them.''

"The canebrake country?" Dusty turned to look at the Kid. "You allow to take those mules through there?"

"I've run mules through the canebrakes," Conway said dubiously. "But never a bunch this size."

"Reckon there's always a start for everything," the Kid replied. "How long have you been using that string?"

"Three, four years. But never all of them at one whirl like we're doing now."

"And they will follow that bell mare of your'n?"

"Never lose her."

The Kid nodded. He was sure that Mike Conway meant just what he said. The mules were trained to follow the bell mare all the time, unfastened and allowed to pick their own way. However they were rarely used in such large groups as would be necessary to transport the arms and ammunition. That would be their only hope, that the mules would keep moving after the bell mare through the winding trails of the canebreak country. It would be impossible in most places for Conway's outriders to keep on the flanks of the mules and there would be little chance of watching the animals. It said much for Conway's skill as a mule trainer and handler that the Ysabel Kid was willing to risk going through the cane-brakes with the mules.

The following day the huge band of mules, loaded with the bundles of rifles and boxes of ammunition were led out of town before dawn. The Ysabel Kid, Dusty Fog and Alden stayed on until daylight then left town by another trail, riding as if headed along the sea-coast. The Kid circled back to make sure they were not being followed or watched and then took them across country to join Conway's men as they held the mules at the edge of the canebrakes.

It was the first time Alden had ever seen the thick mass of growth and the high cane shoots which formed an unholy tangle.

"Do you think we can get lost there?" Alden asked.

"Happen we don't get lost," the Kid replied comfortingly.

"Which same we don't do, not with the Kid guiding us," Conway put in. "He knows the trails in there like you know New Haven. You couldn't lose him."

Dusty sat silent, watching the others. He was sure that the Ysabel Kid would get them through to the Rio Grande and across it. After that no man could say what would happen next. He had decided that he would go along without Handiman's agent and left a letter with Farron to be sent to the OD Connected where Handiman was staying as a house guest until his return. He could guess that Handiman would be annoyed to know he was going alone but Dusty was not worried. This was his mission and he would rather handle it his own way for he'd got help from that very able young man the Ysabel Kid and with these rifles he could make a deal with Juarez for the safe passage of the Sheldon Men.

"Let's go then," he said at last. "Move out."

Mike Conway and the Kid rode with Alden and Dusty now, at the head of the line as they went forward, then thinned into single file as the Kid rode through a narrow gap in the bamboo canes. Dusty came second, Alden third and Conway brought up the rear followed by a mare with a bell fastened round her neck. This was the bell-mare and the mules were trained to follow her; in the dark they would keep in touch with the sound of the bell and this was what the Kid was counting on now. The mules were strung out nose to tail behind them in a long line and he hoped that their training and instinct would keep them moving for long enough to get them through the thickest of the canebrakes.

Once inside the canebrakes they were surrounded and enclosed by the thick growing bamboo intersected by other narrow or wider trails which cut off from or across the one they were following. Alden was hopelessly lost inside a couple of minutes and although Dusty retained his sense of direction for a short time after Alden, he also soon knew that left alone he would have very serious trouble in ever finding his way out again.

Riding his dun behind Alden, Mike Conway looked around him at the very sameness of the clumps of bamboo, one looking just like the next and every hundred yards looking like the last hundred or the hundred ahead. It was a bewildering and scaring feeling, even to a man who'd gone through the Canebrakes before. Conway was a smuggler and a good one but he mostly tried to avoid this sort of country. He'd been through it with small groups of mules at times, but only when forced to by dire necessity and then only with an Indian guide who knew the trails. Never had he been so deeply in as they were now going.

The Kid alone appeared calm and relaxed as he rode at the head of the party. His Winchester rifle was across his knees and his red-hazel eyes never missed a thing. His Comanche blood gave him an inborn instinct to remember any trail he ever rode and never did an instinct stand him so much good use as now. He pushed on at an even pace, allowing the big white stallion to pick its own way along and knowing the horse would make for the river even if he should get lost. He wanted to get them out there on the banks of the Rio Grande before night and if possible across the other side where the trail widened out for some way ahead, though still winding and no easy route to follow. The Kid looked back over his shoulder and called to Conway to get a count made of the mules. There was no delay in doing this and Dusty himself stayed where the trail started to widen to count the mules as they went by. He watched them pass, counting in the same manner he'd learnt to count a herd of cattle as they moved by him. This was far easier than making a trail count for the mules came along singly and there was not so many of them as to make the use of a cord to tally the number of hundreds necessary.

Despite the small number Dusty was pleased to see that they had not lost a mule so far. Conway's men, riding at the rear of the group grinned amiably at Dusty and one asked, "How's it going up there, Cap'n?"

"Good enough," Dusty replied. "We haven't lost any yet."

"Hope we don't. If we got separated down here, I don't know when we'd get back together again."

Dusty thought the same thing himself as he turned his paint and headed back the way he'd just come. He rode by the mules and felt more than relieved when he saw Conway and the bell-mare ahead of him. It wasn't until he was back alongside the Kid again that he felt completely at ease. The narrow trails down in the canebrakes weren't for him. He much preferred the open range country where a man could see his way along. This country was too secretive for him.

"How's it back there?" the Kid asked. "We still got any left?"

"Couple," Dusty replied. "Fact being we haven't lost one so far."

"Didn't expect to," the Kid waved a hand round. "Mules are smart critters, real smart. They don't like this sort of range and they'll stay bunched until we get out of here. That's why we're going to keep moving. There are a couple of clearings ahead and the graze is good. I want to push across them as fast as we can. If the mules get the idea they can find food there they'll balk and we'll be stuck with them."

Conway caught up as the Kid talked and agreed with all the young man said. He knew his mules would follow the bell-mare but that if they once got stopped in what they regarded as a nice safe area they would be hard to move. He couldn't see any way they might be able to avoid it except by doing what the Kid suggested, and keeping the mules moving.

The first of the clearings lay ahead of them, an open space not more than a hundred yards across but nearly half a mile long and offering good grazing. Even as the men came into view there was a rush of hooves and several wild steers went crashing into the canebrakes at the other side.

"Keep them moving," the Kid yelled as the bell-mare led her followers. "Don't let them get their heads down and grazing."

Dusty sent his paint hurling forward, swinging his rope and urging the mules on by him. He knew they were far harder to drive than cattle and that if they once took it into their heads to stop it would be a hard task starting them again. The bell-mare went on, her bell ringing as she stepped out across the open and the mules followed her, crowding out into the open. The Conway men kept their charges moving at a fair speed and they were across the open space before any of them realised it was there. Back into the narrow trail again there was less chance of a mule balking when it followed the tail of the animal in front and was crowded in by the one behind.

They travelled on, walking the horses and leading them in the cavalry manner instead of riding all the time. There were few delays; once a pack came loose along the line and Conway's men cut their way through the bamboo to get alongside and readjust the load. Later a big, old black bear challenged their right to use the path, snorting and grunting as it reared back on its hind legs and waved the forefeet with the long, curved claws in defiance.

"No shooting," Dusty warned as the Kid's rifle lifted. "We may have fooled the French but they'll surely get suspicious if they hear shooting from in here."

The Kid nodded. He knew that the sound of shooting would carry far. Yet he did not wish to stop the line as the back part of it was still in the last of the clearings. The horses were snorting and jibbing back now, fiddle-footing restlessly as the black bear went down on his four feet again and stood shaking his head slowly from side to side and growling.

Dusty suddenly dug the spurs into his big paint stallion causing it to leap forward. The horse was used to hunting bears and the scent of one didn't scare the paint as badly as it was doing the mount Alden was afork. The big paint stallion hurled forward right at that old bear. Dusty shook loose his rope and swung it over his head then with a shattering Rebel warwhoop brought the hondo of the rope round and down, lashing full on to the tip of the bear's nose.

That old bear was the master of the canebrakes. He'd grown old and ornery in there, the undisputed ruler of all he surveyed. Never had any creature, not even a longhorn bull come at him in that manner. It shook him back on to his heels, then the yell jarred his nerves even more and when the stinging pain assailed his nose he decided he'd taken all he meant to. With a half snort, half grunt he whirled and went up that trail like the devil after a yearling. Dusty followed him lashing with the rope and yelling wildly. The old bear made a new record for a fast departure into the safety of the cane-brake thicket where he mostly lay up.

Bringing the paint to a halt Dusty looked round and grinned back at the Kid who was still riding at an even pace towards him. Taking his bandana out the Ysabel Kid wiped sweat from his face, his grin a mite weak.

"Don't you ever do nothing like that again, Dusty," he said. "I ain't never seen anyone fool enough to charge a b'ar afore."

"Don't reckon that ole bear had either," Dusty answered. "I figgered he might light out if somebody came at him. He wouldn't expect it."

The Kid shook his head, eyeing Dusty with new respect. Among the Comanches the bear was regarded as being a dangerous enemy and one to be avoided. He would no more thought of charging at that bear with only a rope than he would of going into the United States Customs Office and declaring a load of contraband. Dusty Fog rose even higher in the Kid's estimation.

Dusty rode on with his friend, watching the expression on that usually immobile and unemotional face. He knew that both Hondo Fog and Ole Devil Hardin could find use for the talents of a man like the Ysabel Kid and hoped that when this business in Mexico was over his newfound friend would want to come back with him. The Kid was alone now, his smuggler band broken and separated after the death of Sam Ysabel. They might or might not come back together if the Kid wanted them but Dusty hoped they would refuse. The Kid was an amiable and handy young man but he was follow-ing an illegal profession and Dusty knew that sooner or later he would come into conflict with the law. There would be shooting for the Kid was not the sort to accede tamely to having his stock-in-trade taken from him. From then on the Ysabel Kid would be on the run and on a downgrade with a pull on him which would drive him deeper and deeper into crime. All too well Dusty knew that there was no single level of crime. Once in a man it grew worse until there was no hope for him.

The mules moved on and as night came down they could hear the gentle murmur of running water. The ground opened out ahead of them and Dusty brought his horse to a halt, looking around him.

"The Rio Grande?" he asked pointing to where water glinted between the trees.

"Unless somebody snuck in and changed it for the North Canadian," the Kid answered.

Dusty ignored this and went on, "Reckon Mike could hold the line here while we take a pasear around?"

"Sure, why?"

"Just a hunch. Was I the French Commander I'd not let the wagons fool me too much. I'd get to figgering that a man'd be loco to come down to a ford that was being watched. So I'd figure that maybe the man I wanted was expecting me to think the wagons would go some other way and I'd have patrols out."

"Could be," the Kid agreed. "But it ain't all that likely. They don't know about the mules yet. Sure, they've likely got a man watching around Brownsville but Mike never brought the mules into town. Allow we've got us a day or so until we have anyone after us."

They rode from the shelter of the big river; the Kid at the right, his Winchester resting on his knee, muzzle in the air. At the left Dusty sat his big paint with the short carbine on his arm. He'd chosen that weapon in the face of the Kid's arguments that it was too small and wouldn't have much better range than the revolver. To Dusty the new Henry in its carbine form was the ideal saddle weapon. Short, compact, light and carrying twelve bullets which could be thrown out as fast as any man would ever need. With arms like this his troop of the Texas Light Cavalry would have been able to stir up the Yankees even more than they had managed when armed with just revolvers. The carbine nestled in the crook of Dusty's arm as he rode forward alert and watchful.

Here the Rio Grande levelled down to a gentle flow over a firm gravel bottom and allowed an easy passage not afforded at most other places for some fifty miles in either direction. The ford was not known to many men and fewer still knew how to find it. On both sides of the river the country was thick and awkward to travel over, the canebrakes on the American side and dense woods on the other. There were many men, members of the United States Customs included, who swore there was no way a man could cross the Rio Grande for a hundred or more miles between the two main fords. The Indians knew of this ford and how to get to it; few others knew but the Ysabel Kid, grandson of Chief Long Walker of the Comanches knew it. He also knew that the secret of the ford was safe. Mike Conway might like to use it again but would never chance it for he could never find his was through the canebrakes.

They crossed the ford and made a thorough search through the woods but found no sign of any life. On the way back the Kid told Dusty that he knew of at least two more of these secret fords along the Rio Grande and there might be more.

"We'll halt here for the night," the Kid told Conway and Alden when they all met. "Rest up here and cross in the morning. The country is rough over there but not as bad as the brakes here. We'll go through it in daylight and cover as much distance as we can. After that we'll just have to see what we can do."

Conway nodded. "Might be best to move after dark," he suggested.

"Might be at that," Dusty agreed. "But there is one thing wrong with it. If the French hear this many mules moving at night they'll surely know something is wrong. They'll know no man would be moving so big a bunch after dark unless he was trying to keep out of the way."

"What do you reckon then, Dusty?" the Kid asked.

"We move in daylight and try to bluff any French we see. If Lon rides ahead as scout we can get word if the French are coming. If they do I'll get my uniform out and we'll be some of the boys riding for the French. If we can bluff through all right. If we can't—"

"Yes?" Alden asked.

"Ole Juarez is going to be some ammunition short when we get the rifles to him."

CHAPTER SEVEN

A Student of the Art of Bowie

THE crossing of the Rio Grande offered no great difficulty for the mules were all long used to making these fords. Mike Conway watched the last of his animals coming ashore and shook his head.

"Tell you, Cap'n Fog," he said looking back, "If I hadn't been along on this ride I wouldn't have believed it could be made."

"We're not out of the woods yet, Mike," Dusty warned. "It's a long ride to Monterrey and it'll be longer if the French know we've come across here."

The mules were moved out again with Dusty and the Kid ranging out ahead of them, riding under the rims and watching every inch of ground ahead of them. For all their caution they saw no sign of French soldiers all the first day.

"Got company, Dusty," the Kid remarked.

Dusty looked up from his place by the small fire. Twenty or more Mexicans sat their horses on a rim looking down at them. They were a varied bunch, some wearing uniforms, most of them not. The Kid felt relieved to see that the small thin faced man in the centre of the group wore the uniform of Colonel in the Juarez army. The others might be *guerillos* but that one was a professional soldier and would hold the others in check.

"Stand fast all of you," Dusty ordered. "Tom, you and Lon best do the talking while the rest of us cover you."

"Cover us but keep the rifles down," the Kid replied. "I'll talk to them but if any of them try to lift a gun shoot fast."

The Ysabel Kid and Alden rode forward towards the Mexicans. The Kid was alert for trouble. He knew those *guerillos.*, they were no better than bandits most of them. This bunch here did not look any better or worse than the others, and only the fact that there were a couple of soldiers along stopped the Kid from fighting right away.

"*Saludos,*" the Kid lifted his hand as he looked at the Mexicans.

"Who are you?" the big, hard-faced burly man seated next to the small officer asked. "What are you doing here?"

"Picking blueberries," the Kid answered, then to the Mexican officer, "We are looking for Juarez."

"You are, huh!" the big man sneered. "I suppose you and the rest of—"

"Charro, I'm in command here," the small man roared. "Keep your mouth shut. And you, *señor,* what do you want with Juarez?"

"Come down and talk with us, *señor.*"

The Mexican looked hard at the Kid's young face, wondering where so young a gringo learned to speak such fluent Spanish. Having come from the south of Mexico Colonel Chavez did not know the Ysabel Kid even by repute.

"We will come."

The men rode down the slope into the camp area and swung down from their horses then gathered round the cook fire when Conway's cook started to hand out the food that remained from his morning cooking spell. The Mexicans for the most part accepted the hospitality with grins of friendship for they like their leader came from the south and were not used to gringos. Nor had they the heritage of warfare the northern men shared with the *Americanos del Norte.* Only Charro seemed to be determined to cause trouble for he growled sullen complaints about the food and the coffee.

"May I ask what is in the boxes?" Chavez asked.

"Repeating rifles for Juarez," the Kid replied and drew the new Henry from his saddleboot. "Rifles like this one."

"Like that?" there was reverence in the Mexican's voice for he had never seen such a rifle as this one.

"Just like it."

Charro lurched forward. "We have heard of no such rifles."

"Juarez does not tell his men everything," Dusty put in; something about the big Mexican annoyed him.

Charro spun round, noted the small Texan's apparent youth and innocence and reached out a hand to put it on to Dusty's chest meaning to push him backwards. Faster than the eye could follow Dusty moved. What he did was absurdly simple but the result was spectacular. His hands linked together on the back of the Mexican's dirty hand, flattening it to his chest. Then he dropped to his right knee and pain knifed through Charro's arm. He was brought to his knees by the pain and by the fact that if he did not go down his wrist would snap. Dusty let loose and brought his knee up under the other's jaw lifting him up and on to his back.

Charro landed hard, his hand clawing at his gun. Colonel Chavez stepped in and his foot came down hard on Charro's wrist, holding his hand still. "Look, *cabron*. Look and thank me for saving your life."

Charro looked. The small Texan stood with a gun in his left hand, the hammer eared back under his thumb. Even as the big Mexican looked the gun went back into leather again and the hand lifted clear.

Chavez smiled mockingly and stepped clear; he was not too fond of Charro from the way he acted. "So these rifles are for Juarez?" he asked.

"They are," it was Alden who spoke.

Charro got to his feet and scowled at Dusty but kept clear of the young man. However he was clearly aiming to try and make trouble. "I say they are for the French, not for Juarez," he growled.

"If they are for the French why would we bring them

through the canebrakes like this?'' the Kid sneered. "Even a loco bobo like you can see that we would be well escorted and on the main trail if these were for the French."

"Who are you?" Charro snarled.

"They call me *el Cabrito*."

"El Cabrito?" Chavez asked and there was a mumble of talk among his men for that name had reached even down to Oaxaca Province in the far south.

"El Cabrito?" Charro sneered. "The man they say never misses with his rifle. Who can move in the bush like a ghost and who can use a knife better than any man in Mexico. You tell us that your are *el Cabrito*?"

The Kid faced Charro looking meaner than all hell and Comanche savage enough to scare most men. His voice fell to a deep-throated Comanche grunt as he asked:

"You doubt my word, *pelado*?"

The other's face hardened, yet he was cautious for he knew that the Kid spoke truly. "I say they lie and we should kill them all, then take the rifles."

"You talk big, *pelado*," the Ysabel Kid sneered, "but when it comes to talk of fighting it is we should do, not I should do."

"What do you mean?"

"I'm going to prove I'm *el Cabrito*. May you live to enjoy it."

The Kid advanced until he stood with his back to the half-circle of grim faced gringos. He held his rifle in one hand, the other extracting a Mexican silver dollar from his pocket. Without looking he threw it over his shoulder and called "Dusty!"

Dusty caught the coin and tossed it into the air. It went up in a flickering turning arc and as it reached the peak spun off course. The Kid came round in a smooth turn, his rifle leaping into his shoulder and the eyes lining it even as his turn completed. One shot crashed out—one lone shot, taken almost before the Kid came to a halt in his turn. But fast taken or not, the bullet flew true and the coin was hit and knocked away to land at the feet of Colonel Chavez.

The Kid levered out the empty case and picked it up for reloading, then gave his attention to the Mexicans who were looking at his smoking rifle with awe. Not one of them would have believed any man could make such a shot. With the old muzzle-loading single-shot weapons they carried none could have hoped to hit the coin even if it was still.

With a mocking smile on his face the Kid turned to Charro and said: "Now, let's see how you can shoot."

"You shoot well," Chavez remarked. "How are you with a knife?"

The Kid slid back his rifle into his saddleboot, then unfastened the pigging thong from the bottom of his holster. He unbuckled the belt and swung it in his left hand.

"I will give you proof. This *pelado,*" he indicated Charro, "insulted me. We will go into the bush thirty yards apart and armed with knives. Only one of us will return. Will that satisfy you?"

Chavez smiled, his white teeth flashing. "It will. Charro, remove your gunbelt and prepare."

Charro gulped. This was not going the way he'd hoped it would. He'd expected Chavez and the other men to fall in with his idea of killing the gringos and taking the rifles to be sold to Juarez by themselves. Now he was to have no choice. He must face this gringo boy in the bush there with a knife. If he won Chavez would listen to him. If he lost, there would be no need for him to worry over anything.

"I am prepared," he said, swinging off the gunbelt and passing it to Chavez then drawing the long bladed, double edged knife from its bootsheath. It was a long and evil-looking weapon and with it in his hand he turned to face the dark boy he was to fight.

There was a knife in the hand of the Ysabel Kid and what a knife. Eleven and a half inches of razor sharp steel, almost two and a half inches across at the guard with the convex curve of the sharpened lower edge meeting the convex curve of the upper edge exactly in the centre of the knife. The convex edge was also sharpened to the same razor edge, but the straight piece which ran from it to the guard was rounded and thick for strength. That was the knife of the Ysabel Kid, a real, genuine, James Black bowie from the same forge the old Texas master's own blade came and made to his own specifications. The finest fighting knife ever devised, manufactured or used by man.

For a moment Charro looked at the long and wicked knife in the hand of the Texan. He licked his lips for he now knew he was faced by *el Cabrito* and there was no escape from a fight. Chavez and the other men would never agree to his not fighting now.

"Come, Charro. We don't want to be here all day," Chavez snapped. "Take your place and I will give the signal."

Dusty escorted the Kid thirty yards along the track at the edge of the thick bush. They stood side-by-side and watched Chavez push Charro into place facing them.

"Hope you know what you're doing, *amigo*," Dusty remarked.

"I know. I've seen that *hombre* before. He was one of Giss's pards. They won't take my word for it but when I've done with him he'll talk loud, long and often."

"Are you ready, *señor*?" Chavez called.

"Ready, willing and able!" the Kid replied.

"Then go!"

Charro whirled and plunged into the thick bush fast, running forward to dive under a bush and lay there. At the same moment the Ysabel Kid shook his knife and gave voice to a Comanche war-scream and went in after him in a smooth dive. Where Charro halted and took cover the Kid hunted for him knowing what the Mexican was doing and willingly matching Comanche skill and training against a dangerous and passive enemy. It was his favourite game and one at which he was willing to match his skill with any man, white, brown or red. Whithout a move that would make a sound he flitted through the woods, a black dressed shadow with a razor sharp Bowie knife in his hand.

Charro lay under the comparative safety of the bush, hugging the ground and trying to see some sign of the black dressed, baby-faced killer who even now was stalking him. He knew that *el Cabrito* would never lay up passively and wait for the other man to come for him but would be hunting and questing as dangerous as any cougar and more willing to attack.

From his hiding place under his waist-band the Mexican drew a Derringer pistol and grinned savagely as he hefted the heavy little single shot weapon. He would rather have been holding a sixshooter but could never have concealed one from the eagle scrutiny of Colonel Chavez and Chavez was too much of a gentleman to let Charro bring a known firearm into a knife duel. It was having this Derringer which gave him the confidence to come in here and risk meeting the Ysabel Kid in combat. It gave an advantage over even the finest knife-fighter, for the bowie knife was outranged by the comparatively short-ranged weapon as a Derringer.

Minutes rolled by, minutes which brought sweat running down Charro's face and made him repeatedly loosen his grip on the Derringer and wipe dry his palm. He was afraid and wished that he was not in a place where he could only make an exit in one direction. However the Kid must be near now, prowling through the bush like a hunting mountain lion. Any sign or sound Charro made would be transmitted in the uncanny silence of the woods to the keen ears which sought for such things.

For a brief instance he thought he saw a black shadow flit across an open space, but there was no sound and he decided his imagination was playing tricks on him.

Then from close at hand a bird gave a startled squawk and rocketed up into the air. Charro twisted to where the sound came from, bringing the Derringer cracking out even before he was round.

From behind there came a sudden rush of feet, even as a branch fell from the bush above Charro where the Kid threw it to make a diversion. Charro tried to come round and his ears were jarred by the hideous, unnerving scalpscream of a Comanche dog soldier. He was almost round when he saw a black dressed shape hurling at him. A face as savage as any

Comanche loomed before him, then he crashed down and felt the numbing agony as the great knife lashed round biting through coat, shirt, flesh and muscle. The knife came back and blood spurted into the air.

Men crashed through the bushes, coming fast to investigate the shot which should not have come. Dusty was the first to arrive on the scene and he came with his guns out. He holstered the long-barrelled Colts and stepped forward to where the Kid was standing looking down at Charro.

"What happened?" Chavez came up.

"The *pelado* had a gun," the Kid replied.

"He lies, Colonel," Charro gasped. "I fought fairly, he shot me then cut me to hide the hole."

"So?" Chavez looked hard at the Kid, then back at Charro. "One is lying. I wonder which. Well?"

A Mexican stepped forward and saluted; it was to him Chavez spoke. "I saw Charro with the gun two days ago."

The Kid bent down and lifted the Derringer up to examine it. He turned the gun over and over in his hands, then grinned mirthlessly. "Where did you get this gun from?" he asked.

Charro looked up with fear in his eyes as he tried to staunch the flow of blood which came from his wound. He licked his lips and shook his head weakly. The Kid pulled his hair and dragged the head back, placing the edge of his knife to the neck.

"Why do you ask?" Chavez inquired. "Do you know it?"

"Sure, there were a pair of them owned by a couple of hombres called Giss 'n' Kraus. They used them to identify their men when they were smuggling. They'd give one to buyer and the other to the man with the goods. This is one of the two guns."

"I see, but Kraus is our man; he works for Juarez."

"Sure." The Kid turned the gun over and carved on the trigger-guard was the word, "Giss".

"Giss. He is the Maximillian man who nearly trapped Almonte and Bonaventura. What does this mean?"

Charro was too far gone to reply to the question. He

slumped back against the tree, bleeding to death as the other men talked. Not one of them showed any sign of helping him until Dusty bent down and examined the gaping wound and started to tie a tourniquet around the arm.

"Tell you what it means," the Kid replied. "Giss and Kraus are still in cahoots. They're working for the French but Kraus acts like he is on your side. Then when he gets anything to pass on to the French he sends Charro with it and that gun acts as a blab board for him."

Chavez could speak some English but the term "Blab board" had him beaten. It was Dusty who explained that a blab board was the sheet of cowhide carrying his ranch's brand the spread rep. wore to announce who he belonged to at a round-up. Dusty also explained that Charro would carry the Derringer for a passport to show any French he contacted that he was to be trusted by them.

"So?" Chavez growled, lowering the muzzle of the revolver he drew. "Die, dog!"

The bullet cut over the Kid's shoulder and Charro's body bounced as the lead smashed into his head. He quivered once and went limp. The Kid rose, eyeing Chavez in an unpleasant manner.

"What the hell?" he growled.

"So die all traitors."

"Real nice and patriotic, friend." In his annoyance the Kid forgot to speak Spanish. "But I'd surely rather had him alive and talking than dead and dumb. I wanted to know just where I could find Kraus."

"I am sorry, my young friend. I did not know you had private business with him or I would have held off. It is to be regretted that he died so easily. I acted hastily, something no soldier should do. Come, we will leave this place."

The men returned through the trees, none of them saying much—Alden and Conway having stayed behind to watch the weapons showed their relief when Dusty and the Kid came back with the Mexicans.

"What happened?" Alden asked.

Dusty explained quickly and then gave the order to prepare

to move out and head towards Monterrey. The mule skinners went to work loading up the mules with either boxes or long bundles. Conway's men worked fast for there was a large number of animals to load. Each mule was given its balanced load, one bundle of rifles or two boxes of ammunition strapped to each pannier and fastened on with the hitch which held it securely.

When all the mules were ready to move on Chavez came up and looked round. "My men and I will ride with you to Monterrey." he said. "It will be best for all concerned and I think Benito would want it."

"Why sure," Dusty agreed. He grinned cheerfully as he waved the men to move on. "Besides with only a thousand of these repeaters among the Juarez army a man will need to be on hand to make sure he gets at least one of them."

Chavez smiled back. This small, soft talking gringo who seemed to be the leader of the men was a smart one. Chavez could tell a born leader and knew that here was one, such a one as the small, half Indian Benito Juarez who would soon rule all Mexico and even now led the fight for freedom against the French.

"Lon, take a point," Dusty ordered, then turned to Chavez. "Sorry, Colonel. As senior officer you take command of the escort."

"I accept your judgment, Jose, ride with *el Cabrito* as the scout."

Chavez watched the Ysabel Kid and one of his half-Indian men head out fast to scout the area ahead, then he turned to Dusty and asked who the small Texan rode for, thinking him to be a member of the United States Army.

"Texas Light Cavalry. I retired at the end of the War."

They rode side-by-side, Alden staying back with Conway and the muleskinners. For a time Chavez was silent as they followed the scouts, keeping under cover as well as they could all the time, and avoiding skylines.

"The Texas Light Cavalry were Confederate Army?" There was suspicion in the soft spoken inquiry.

"Sure."

"There are many Confederate men riding for Maximillian."

"I'm not gainsaying it," Dusty could almost read the Mexican's thoughts. "That is why I am helping take these rifles to Juarez."

"That is strange, very strange. I would have thought you would be taking these weapons to your friends."

"Nope, to Juarez. You know that the United States Government is willing to help your people against the French?"

"There was some rumour."

"No rumour, Colonel. It's the living truth. Do you think Washington would've allowed us to leave the country with these rifles if they were aiming to help the French?"

"It doesn't appear likely," Chavez agreed. "Why then are you coming?"

"I want to ask Juarez to give the Confederate soldiers free and unrestricted passage back to the United States. Then I aim to go down and talk with General Sheldon, their leader, and get him to come home with me. That way our country will be free to help you without causing international trouble."

"I see."

The Kid and Jose were at the top of a rim, just below the skyline. The Kid turned in his saddle and removed his hat to wave it round his head. Dusty twisted in his saddle and brought the line of mules to a halt. Then he rode up the hill with Conway, Chavez and Alden following him.

The Kid and the Mexican were down from their horses and laying just under the rim looking over. Dusty swung down from his paint and left it standing with the reins hanging loose. He drew the carbine and went up the slope to drop by the Kid.

On the other side of the slope, riding in a course which would traverse their own came horsemen. Dusty did not need the tricolour flag carried by one of the men to know that here were French cavalry. A strong company by American standards, over sixty men, with scouts ahead, on the flanks behind them.

Chavez joined Dusty, he also watched the Frenchmen, noting their scouts rode across the trail at the bottom of the slope that started the long climb up this side.

"They will see us, there is no chance of hiding so many mules," he said softly. "We must make a fight."

"Against a force that strong?" Dusty objected. "We wouldn't have a chance."

"With the repeating rifles we would."

"Sure and the second volley would warn the French that we were armed with repeaters." Dusty shook his head. "It's no good that way, Colonel. The French know about these rifles but they don't know for certain they are in Mexico. Half a minute after we open fire they will know and they'll know how we're moving them. Then they'll light out of here faster'n a Neuces steer and tell the main force what's happened to the rifles."

"Dusty's right," the Kid agreed. "The French allow we're trying to bring the rifles by wagon, not by mule. We want to keep them thinking that way as long as we can. We won't do it by fighting them bunch with the repeaters. They'll surely come over here and some of them will see the mules."

"You're right. But they will see us when they reach the top of the slope and no officer would ride by such a sight."

Chavez moved back down the slope, signalling to his men to come up and join him. "We go over that slope and fight the French. Move the mules and tell Juarez I die for my country."

Before Dusty or the others could say a word Chavez and his men were riding up the slope. The Colonel turned and raised a hand in a salute then riding as if on a routine patrol led his men over and down the other side.

"Move them out, fast!" Dusty ordered.

"I'm going back to see what happens," the Kid growled.

Dusty caught the black sleeve and gripped it hard, meeting his friend's eyes. "Chavez knew what he was doing. Don't try and help him with that repeater."

For a time, until the mule train was nearly out of sight, the

Kid stayed and watched the gallant but hopeless fight. He longed to go down and help but knew that to do so would cause the very thing Chavez led his men to prevent.

CHAPTER EIGHT

Mark Counter Changes Sides

THEY pushed the mules hard, keeping the loping animals moving at a fair speed and putting distance between them and Chavez's fighting men. For a time Dusty rode at the point of the line then he let Conway go ahead as scout and cut back for the rear. They were travelling through the rolling Mexican hill country and from the top of a rim Dusty sat his paint watching the big white stallion bringing the Ysabel Kid towards him. Faintly in the distance he could still hear shooting and knew that Chavez still fought the French, holding them from finding the tracks of the mules and giving Conway's train a chance to get well clear.

The Ysabel Kid looked Indian-savage as he came up, bringing the big white stallion to a rump-sliding halt and scowling at Dusty.

"We could have helped them," he said.

"Sure, and the French would have known about these rifles. Do you reckon I liked leaving them to fight?"

"Nope, don't reckon you did. It galls a man to miss a fight though."

Dusty gripped his friend's arm again. The grip was firm and his eyes were friendly as he said, "Sure I know how you feel. Come on, we'd best catch up with the others."

The mule train was kept moving all that day and the next. It was only a three-day drive from Monterrey to Texas, going by the most direct route but they did not travel direct. Once they spent three hours hid in a bosque while a French patrol cooked a meal less than half a mile from them. The French were not alert or even expecting trouble for they ignored the sudden bray of one of the mules. Another time they were forced to make a long detour through the safe cover at the bottom of a dried-up river-bed to avoid the eyes of another patrol.

On the third day the Ysabel Kid announced to Dusty that he would head for a small town called San Juanita and see a few friends, who would know if the French were about. Dusty wasn't too happy about letting the Kid ride alone but knew that he himself could not leave the train and that the Kid would prefer to go unescorted.

So the Kid rode ahead of the others, travelling at a better speed than they could make with the loaded-down animals. He rode with the caution of a Comanche on a scouting mission, sticking to cover, surveying the ground ahead and never moving over a rim without first making a careful approach and study from under it. He halted the horse on the rim above San Juanita, which was more of a village, and a small village at that. It consisted of some thirty mud and adobe built houses, none of them large, a slightly larger adobe built of cantina and a small stone church. The town was surrounded on three sides by well-wooded land, but on this side from where the Kid was approaching it was all fairly open country. Halfway along was a tall, flat-topped rock which overlooked the surrounding countryside and in the days when contraband was being run into San Juanita provided a very handy place for a man to sit and watch the surrounding district. From the top of the rock a man could see every inch of the land from it down to the town and well over the thick wooded country with the only two paths through the woods in plain view. Another thing about that rock was that it was unclimbable except from the side nearest the town, where someone had taken time and cut steps into the steep face allowing a man to get up in a hurry, or down again.

The Kid rode by Lookout Rock as it was called and down towards the town. He frowned as he studied the deserted streets. San Juanita was never a busy place, that is, not in the day time, though it could get very busy after dark, but there were usually a few people in sight. It was not yet the hour of siesta either and the very stillness would have warned the Kid if it had been any other place. But San Juanita, tucked away in the hills as it was, never attracted any attention to it and there were men who'd ridden past it on the other side of the slope who would have sworn no village existed there.

The street was empty and deserted, and the Kid wondered where his friends were as he rode in along it. Even if the men were asleep in the houses and the women not talking to each other they should have kept someone watching the trail.

Halting his stallion the Kid looked round then called, "Hey Ruis, Pablo. Come on out here!"

"Raise your hands and drop your guns!"

The voice was speaking Spanish, not pure Spanish but with the same accent the men in Brownsville had used. The Kid sat his horse and lifted his hands to shoulder height seeing three rifles lined on him from different hiding places. To move would be death for the men were resting their weapons and not all of them would miss.

A big heavily built man with a hard, coarse face and wearing the uniform of the French Blue Hussars stepped from a hut. In his hand he held a Lefauchex pistol and on his sleeve the three bars of a sergeant.

"Get down and remove that gunbelt," he ordered.

The Kid swung down from his saddle, knowing that he would never escape by a fast dash for he'd looked round and there were many rifles lined on him now. Then even as his foot touched the floor he realised he must not let them get his horse for in the saddleboot was a rifle of a kind the French would never have seen before. Any doubt they had as to his identity would be settled when they examined the rifle as they were sure to. Mere curiosity would call for a closer look and no soldier could resist examining so novel a weapon closer. Along the top of the barrel was printed the words, "Winchester Repeating Firearms Company, New Haven, Conn." He guessed the French would know which company were selling

the arms to Juarez and would have warned their men to be on
the lookout for such weapons.

Slowly he lowered his hands to unbuckle the heavy gunbelt. He swung it from his wrist and lowered it to the ground.
Then he hissed a command. The big white stallion rocketed
forward, leaping into a racing stride which took every man by
surprise. The men were concentrating on the Ysabel Kid and
when the horse went off like that they were confused, not
knowing if they should still cover the man or shoot the horse.

The sergeant was in no doubt. His Lefauchex gun came up
and crashed but it would have taken a better pistol shot than
he to hit that racing white stallion. ''Stop it!'' he bellowed.
''Don't let it—!''

It was too late. The big white was running fast and even
as the men poured out of the houses they were too late for the
horse was out of town and streaking back the way it came.

The sergeant watched the horse go, then turned and looked
at the tall, dark and innocent looking young man who stood
watching him with mocking eyes. ''Pig!'' he snarled and
lashed the back of his hand across the Kid's face.

The young man staggered back; a soldier smashed the butt
of his carbine into the base of his spine sending him forward
again into another crashing blow which sent him to the
ground. The sergeant snarled out strange and savage curses
as he came in drawing his foot back for a kick.

A tall man had come from a house at the shot. He came
forward now, thrusting through the crowd as if it wasn't
there. His left hand shot out, gripped the big sergeant by the
arm, turned him and then the right fist drove out to crash on to
the jaw of the Frenchman hard enough to stretch him flat on
his back.

The Kid looked up at his rescuer, a handsome young,
blond giant. Three or more inches over six foot he stood, with
great wide shoulders that tapered down to a narrow waist and
powerful straight legs. On his head was an expensive Confederate campaign hat, shoved back from his curly, golden
blond hair. The face was very handsome, classic in its shape
and form. He wore the single gold braid from the cuff of his

sleeve to the bend of the elbow and the half-inch wide, three-inch long gold bar at his collar that denoted he was a first Lieutenant but the uniform was not as laid down by Confederate Army Dress Regulations. His double breasted grey tunic did not have the required shirt extending to between hip and knee, but was cut off at the waist. It did have the collar and cuffs of cavalry yellow, but the stand-up collar was open and instead of the required black cravat he wore a tight rolled bandana of scarlet silk, the ends hanging loose almost to his waistband. His trousers were regulation, tight legged and obviously tailored for him, and the shining Jefferson boots were well fitting. Instead of the issue sword belt he wore a buscadero gunbelt with a matched brace of ivory butted Colt 1860 Army revolvers in the low-tied holsters.

All-in-all he looked like a very rich young man who entered the Confederate Army with a commission ready made for him. He also brought with him his own idea of what military uniform should be and wore this variation of it because he preferred it.

The young man might be big but he was neither slow nor clumsy. Behind him one of the men started to raise his rifle, the hammer clicking back under his thumb. The young man came round in a smooth turn, hand dropping and the long-barrelled Colt leaping from his right holster in a fast, proficient draw. The Kid was something of a connoisseur when it came to studying fast draws and this was as fast almost as the draw of his able young friend, Dusty Fog.

"Attention!" a voice snapped.

A tall, dandified young French officer came from the hut where the Confederate made his appearance. He crossed the street with lazy strides, tapping the side of his trousers with his cane. He looked elegant and handsome but there was a hint of cruelty in his face and eyes. He looked round at the men who stood at rigid attention, then at the tall young Confederate lieutenant who was not.

"What is the trouble, Lieutenant Counter?"

"The same as before," the voice was an easy, cultured Texas drawl. "I'm sick of your men ill-treating every living soul that they lay their hands on. This boy hadn't but rode in here when Lefarge jumped him, knocked him down and started to kick him.''

''I see,'' the French officer examined the Ysabel Kid with his cold and cruel eyes. ''This one answers to the description of a man with that firearms seller we heard of.''

''That so?'' Lieutenant Mark Counter looked down without too much interest at the Ysabel Kid. ''He looks some too young for a thing like that. We'd best hang on to him until we get back to Saltillo, but don't ill-treat him any.''

''I'll do what I—''

The French officer's voice died away as the young Texan's hands lifted to hover over the butts of his guns. ''No, you won't, Bardot. Nobody mishandles a prisoner when I'm around.''

''All right.'' Apparently Bardot had quite a fair-sized respect for the Texan's gun skill. He looked back over his shoulder and snapped. ''Take him and tie him up. Throw him in that hut there.''

''No,'' Mark snapped back, looking down at the Kid, ''Here I'll take care of him myself.''

The Kid was no weakling. There was a whipcord strength in his lean frame that was out of keeping with one his size but he was like a baby in the powerful hands of Mark Counter. He was helped to his feet and his gunbelt slung over the big Texan's shoulder. Then Mark pushed the Kid into the small jacal he'd come from to make his timely rescue.

The building was small and of only one room. It was the house of one of the men who'd given good service to the Ysabel family at different times. The house itself gave no sign that the men had a fair amount of money hidden away. It held only a rough table, a couple of chairs and an untidy and dirty looking bed.

Shoving the Kid into one of the chairs Mark fastened him securely and in a way which gave little or no chance of escaping. The Ysabel Kid looked Mark over with fresh respect. The big man might talk like a gentleman and dress like a New Orleans dandy but he knew how to handle rope.

"Sorry I've got to hawgtie you like this, but I've got to make it look real good for when Bardot comes. He's a real mean *hombre* and if he gets his way neither you or I will make Saltillo alive."

"Sure," the Kid watched the handsome face, knowing that he was still alive because of Mark Counter. "What happened to the folks of the town?" he asked.

"There wasn't one of them in sight when we came."

Mark handrolled two smokes, passing one to the Kid and lighting it. He was looking at the Indian dark face and at last asked, "Are you taking rifles to Juarez?"

"Sure."

"You know a lot of Confederate boys are fighting for the French?"—there was a hard note in Mark's voice.

"Sure."

"And you're still taking them?"

"Yep. Cap'n Dusty Fog of the Texas Light Cavalry is with me."

Mark's face showed its disbelief. He knew the reputation of Dusty Fog and could not see that loyal son of Dixie doing any such thing. Mark pulled out the second chair and sat down facing the Kid, his face showing nothing of his feelings. "I can't help you get loose now, boy. Not with you bringing those guns. They're better than anything we've got. I'll see the French don't mistreat you but I'll take you to Saltillo."

For a time the two men stayed silent, each occupied with his thoughts. The door opened and Bardot came in followed by the sergeant. The French officer came over and examined the Kid's bonds carefully, then sniffed and straightened up. He jerked his head and the sergeant left the room.

"Monsieur Counter, I will leave you to guard the prisoner and to make sure he does not escape. I will give instructions to fire upon anyone who comes out."

"Thanks, and when do we eat?"

"I will send *soupe* and coffee across when we make it. Until then you will confine yourself to this hut. I have given orders for a double guard on the horse lines and they have orders to shoot anyone who moves in the street after dark.''

''Sounds like you don't trust somebody,'' the Kid remarked.

Bardot's hand drew back but Mark came to his feet in a lithe move, facing the other man. ''If you want to hit somebody try me. I'm not tied.''

The Frenchman turned on his heel and left the jacal, slamming the door after him. The Ysabel Kid grinned at Mark. ''Looks like we're both prisoners.''

''Man'd say you were right,'' Mark agreed. ''General Bushrod won't be any too pleased when he hears.''

The Kid relapsed into silence for a time, still watching Mark. Then he got more comfortable in the chair and remarked, ''You look a lonely man.''

''Feel it. I never knew just how lonesome until I saw you ride in there on that old range saddle.''

Mark wasn't looking at the Kid. His eyes were on the wall but he was seeing the great rolling Big Bend range country and his father Rance Counter's great R over C ranch. To his ears came the sound of the range, the creaking of saddle leather, the grunting of cowhorses as they worked and the beat of the feet of cattle interspersed with the wild yell of the cowhand. He was tired of this vagrant army life, homesick and wanted to be done with the sort of warfare the French engaged in as they tried to bring the Mexicans to their knees. What he wanted was to head back north, cross the Rio Grande into Texas and feel a comfortable old kak saddle between his knees as he rode the range.

''How'd you like working for the French?'' the Kid asked after a time.

''I don't. I'm surely sick of them and the way they fight. Man, you've never seen such cruel hawgs as they get when they catch a Mexican.''

''You all set to quit them?''

Mark looked at the dark young man for a long time. He rose and went to the door, opening it slightly. The French guard turned, hefting his carbine and nervously easing back the hammer. Shutting the door again Mark returned to the table and sat down again.

"Them, not General Bush."

The Kid was about to speak when the door was opened and two men came in carrying a bowl and a cup each. They put the utensils on the table and turned to go out. Mark looked in at the greyish looking *soupe*, a kind of stew which the French army served at each of its two daily meals. It was nourishing all right but a deadly tedious diet to a man who was as fond of his creature comforts as Mark Counter. He eyed the food with some distaste and went to the door to bellow out for the officer.

Bardot entered. He scowled at Mark and then at the Ysabel Kid. "What now?"

"What am I supposed to do, eat it with my fingers?" Mark replied. "My mess gear is in my saddlebag."

"I will send for it," Bardot watched Mark all the time. There was hatred in his eyes now. Calling to the man outside Bardot gave orders for a couple of spoons to be brought then he stated flatly he would wait until the Kid was tied once more before leaving.

Mark held down his temper, knowing that he could not handle all the patrol at one go even with the aid of the young man they'd captured. He drew the Kid's bowie knife and cut the thongs holding the dark wrists then set to and ate his food. The Kid was hungry now and the soup went down well for he was used to taking what he could get.

With the food done Mark rose and went to the door, pushed by Bardot and stepped outside. The sentry stared at him but made no attempt to raise his carbine for he'd seen just how fast this Texan could draw and with what accuracy he shot even without lifting the guns and looking along their sights. Mark stood there with the Kid's gunbelt hanging over his shoulder still, then he ordered the soldier to fetch his bedroll and turned to go back into the hut.

"Fasten your prisoner again, Monsieur," Bardot ordered. "Then I will leave you to guard him. Remember my orders."

Mark lashed the Kid's arms again, making a thorough job

of it. He went to the dirty window, rubbed it clear and looked out. The town was as deserted in appearance again as if it were a dead town, for Bardot was holding all his men under cover. The horses were picketed out of sight in the woods and under guard so to all signs the village of San Juanita was deserted.

"You said Dusty Fog was riding with you," Mark asked as he returned to the table.

"Why sure."

"What would a reb like him be doing, bringing repeating rifles down here when some of his friends are on the other side?"

"He's come to ask Bushrod Sheldon to come home again," the Kid decided to lay his cards on the table. "Folks up north of the border want him back real bad."

"You reckon he'll go?"

"I reckon he will." The Kid told Mark of the letter Dusty was carrying and the rest of what Dusty told him. "I've seen the letter, and it'll make him go back."

At the end of the narrative Mark rose and paced the room whistling softly an old cattlesong. He knew of both Dusty Fog and Ole Devil Hardin and knew that the latter was probably the only man Bushrod Sheldon would trust. The letter from President Grant might be full of concessions and flowery phrases, but it would have no effect on Bushrod Sheldon unless it was endorsed by a man who he trusted. Mark knew better than the Ysabel Kid the way the battle-weary ex-Confederate veterans who rode for Sheldon felt. Every one of them was tired of this life they led, far from home and family. With anything like a reasonable assurance from the Union Government all would wish to ride north again.

"How about the rifles?" That was the one part of the matter Mark did not like. "Why'd you bring them?"

"For Juarez," the Kid explained, liking this caution and regard for the well-being of his fellows. "See, if the boys do pull out they'll likely have to fight the Mexicans and French all the way north. If we get the guns to Juarez we can get his word the Mexicans will give you boys uninterrupted passage through. That's what Dusty says, and likely he'll be right.''

Mark grinned. He did not know Dusty Fog except by reputation but the ex-Captain must be quite a man if he'd got the Ysabel Kid thinking so highly of him. Suddenly Mark himself was looking forward to meeting the fabulous Dusty Fog who could get all the loyalty and devotion of a dangerous young man like this on so short an acquaintance.

"You trust Juarez?"

"Sure. He'll keep his word and he's got him a real kind way with him for any yahoo who disobeys him. Got a touch of Comanche in him, ole Benito, 'less I miss my guess. If he says you boys can go through no man in his army'll risk disobeying him.''

"I'll let you loose right now and we'll see about getting out of here.''

Mark took the knife and was about to cut the cords when both he and the Kid realised the futility of any escape plan at the moment. The streets were being watched all the time and they would have to run the gauntlet of some twenty or more carbines out in the open with no cover. Not only that but they would also have to cross more open ground before they could get near the horse lines and the guards there were picked for their ability to shoot.

"Maybe best if I leave you tied, I'll loosen the ropes but leave them on. If Bardot found you loose he'd shoot us both down. If not he won't risk it. Only half the patrol are for him, the rest hate him. If he kills me he'll have to have a good excuse or someone will tell General Bush. The French don't want to lose us rebs and they wouldn't like it if one of their officers shot down a Confederate officer without a real good reason.''

"I'll stay tied. I'm comfortable enough.''

"It's a pity your hoss took off like that. We could use him now.''

"He didn't take off, I sent him. He'll have headed back to the mule train and be bringing Dusty Fog along. I don't know what Dusty will do but I figger he won't make a move until after dark. If he doesn't come by midnight I'll get out of here and slide a couple of hosses from the picketline. It won't be hard. I've never seen a Frenchman yet who could keep a decent guard. Which is your hoss?''

''A big bloodbay tied near this end of the line. You can't miss him, he's the biggest hoss there.''

The door opened and Bardot came in, his face showing some triumph. ''I have just received word from Major Duprez that he and his patrol will be joining us here tomorrow. He will arrive late in the afternoon but his advance party will be with us shortly after dawn.'' He stopped for a moment, a sadistic smile on his face as he looked at the Ysabel Kid. ''We will soon know something about you, my friend. Giss is with them.''

CHAPTER NINE

The Rescue

DUSTY FOG was not unduly worried when the Ysabel Kid failed to appear after a couple of hours. He had too much faith in the Indian dark boy to worry for he knew the Kid was going to see friends and might take some time to get back. So Dusty took the point, riding far ahead of the mule train and watching out for any sign of the French as he followed the landmarks the Kid drew for him on a piece of bare soil back at their last camp.

Halting the horse Dusty surveyed the range ahead of him. There was nothing in sight other than the rolling land with its stunted trees and occasional *bosque* of cottonwood, scrub oak and other trees. For all the country ahead Dusty could see there was no sign of human life. He scanned the area with his powerful field-glasses and when satisfied they would be able to travel without risk of ambush waved the slowly moving train up towards him.

Something white flickered into view over a distant hill. It caught Dusty's eye for a brief moment, then disappeared for a moment. The glasses came up once more, sweeping across the range country until they picked up something which made Dusty curse softly under his breath. There were other white horses in Mexico, that he was sure of, but few of them were equipped with a Texas range saddle, fewer with a new model Henry rifle in the saddleboot. And he seriously doubted if there was another horse as big, fast and good looking as that white stallion the Ysabel Kid cheerfully called Nigger.

Mike Conway came alongside Dusty now. The white stallion was closer and still running fast but he recognized it even as had Dusty.

"The Kid's afoot," he said.

Afoot. There were few words in the West so feared as that. In that country of vast, unpopulated miles a horse was more than a means of transport. It was a vital necessity. For a man to be left afoot it was almost certain death.

"Reckon he's hurt bad some place?" Dusty asked.

"Could be. He must have been able to talk. That ole Nigger hoss would stay by him if he wasn't. He must have sent it off."

"That's what I thought." Dusty watched Alden riding up, then pointed to the big white stallion. "The Kid's in bad trouble."

"How many men do you want to go with you?" It was then Alden showed himself to be a true gentleman. He didn't care if the rifles were not delivered, if one of the two young men who'd aided him so much needed help. "Take them and give them a Henry each, take enough bullets as well."

"Thanks, Tom. I won't forget that. But I'd best go alone, I'll have a better chance that way."

Alden shook his head. He watched Dusty starting towards the big white horse which was slowing down now. He looked next at Conway who grinned back at him. "The Cap'n's right, like always. He'll get the Kid back, safe. We'll keep them mules moving towards Monterrey; that's what he wants."

Dusty rode alongside the big white stallion, whispering softly to him, soothing him down, but he did not try to touch him. Dusty looked down at the tracks left by the white. He could read sign fairly well, well enough to follow this line anyhow. Starting the paint forward Dusty found that his tracking ability would not be needed for the white stallion turned and loped ahead of him, only stopping to look back and make sure he was following. Dusty was better than a fair hand with a horse himself and knew the long and patient hours of training it had taken the Ysabel Kid to teach the horse the things it could do.

The white headed back in the direction it had come, travelling at an easy loping stride which the paint could keep up with. Dusty wasted no time in idle speculation as to why the Ysabel Kid had sent the horse, knowing only his friend was in some kind of trouble and that his help was called for. The Kid could have been thrown by the white, but that was not likely. He could have been shot down by the French or anything. All Dusty knew was that his friend was in need of help and he meant to see the need was not left unfulfilled.

For about an hour he rode, then brought the horse to a halt as he looked down on the village of San Juanita. He sat his horse in the same spot the Kid had sat earlier and looked down, then rode towards the big rock. His carbine was in his hands, ready for use as he rode. The village was too still for an afternoon. There should have been some sign of movement down there, people walking the streets and going about their business. Dusty was about to start on down the slope when he saw two men come from one of the huts. He flattened to the side of the rock and then went to his horse and got the glasses from his saddle-pouch. What he saw made him hug the side even more carefully.

The two men crossing the street wore uniform and in colour it could have been either French or Mexican for both went in for blue jackets and red trousers. A closer look told Dusty that these were no Mexicans. The big sergeant had a swarthy face, but not a Mexican look. The other was an officer. His face was definitely not Mexican in feature and far too light. Dusty knew the type, for he'd seen it often enough in New Orleans; the arrogant French Creoles down there had much in common with this elegant officer of the Republic's army.

The two soldiers crossed the street and went to a hut at the near-side. It was then Dusty saw the soldier on guard outside this building and knew the town was full of French soldiers. With his glasses he searched the streets with far greater care, noting enough signs to know that a fair force were hidden in the houses. He also knew that they were cavalry men, the spurs on the sergeant's boots telling him that, and so he searched for their horse lines. His glasses covered the woods behind the town carefully, trying to pierce through the thick cover but not seeing where the horses were hidden. Then he saw a man coming out of the woods, a blue dressed trooper who stood just at the edge, looked towards the town then turned and went back again. He would be one of the picket-line guards looking for a relief. If that had been the Texas Light Cavalry the trooper would have wished he'd never been born deserting his post in that way.

This was not helping Dusty find his friend, although he guessed the Kid was down there in the village, perhaps a prisoner, probably dead. Dusty focused his glasses on the hut again, watching the sergeant standing outside and that the officer had gone in. Then the door opened and the guard turned, half-raising his carbine as a tall man came out. This man was not French but Dusty thought no more of the guard's action than he was of the usual excited French nature. His full attention was on this handsome blond giant who stood at the door. Over one wide shoulder hung a gunbelt with an old Dragoon gun on the holster. Dusty thought he recognised the belt and was sure when the man turned showing the ivory hilted bowie knife at the other side.

That man was a Confederate officer. Dusty knew the Counter version of the official uniform. He did not know Lieutenant Mark Counter except as a very rich and elegant young man whose sartorial taste in uniform was much copied in the deep south cavalry. Dusty's cousin, Red Blaze, had met Mark Counter and copied the style along with many other young officers. Dusty's own uniform was copied from it, with a slightly more official neck fitting. He regarded it as being the best dress for a cavalry man as the skirts of the regulation pattern got in the way.

Dusty watched the Confederate lieutenant return to the hut and shut the door then checked carefully the ground ahead of him making sure that he could find his way in the dark. If the Ysabel Kid was still alive he would be in that hut with the big

Confederate officer. What Dusty could not understand was why the French chose to put a guard on the door as well as the man inside. There was no way of finding out until after dark. So Dusty removed the saddles from both horses, watching the Kid's white all the time. It said much for his horse skill that he managed to remove the saddle with no trouble, for the white would let very few people handle him.

Just before dark Dusty got to his feet and saddled the two horses ready to move. He was finished by the time full blackness came down over the land, the blackness before the moon came out. Then leading the horses Dusty skirted the town and left them as near as he could in the shelter of the woods knowing they would both stay silent. Then he slipped back into the silent deserted town.

Dusty moved along the street, keeping to the dark shadows and hugging the sides of the houses. It was being in so close that let him hear what was being said in one building. He flattened against the side and listened, understanding enough of the fast spoken French to know that the Confederate officer was in deadly peril from the occupants of the building. From what he heard he felt relieved for he gathered they had a prisoner although they harboured homicidal thoughts towards him and the big man who guarded him.

The sentry outside the hut was leaning against the wall, his carbine resting by him in a display of sloppiness that made Dusty's military training and instincts writhe with rage. No man in his outfit would have guarded like that but it was like the French that their men were so lax in the performance of a serious duty like guarding a dangerous prisoner. The sentry's behaviour would be a help now for he appeared to be half asleep and certainly was not in any state to take alert and effective action.

On silent feet Dusty came nearer. He held no weapon, relying on his bare hands to deal with the matter. The French cavalry shako provided too much protection for him to risk dropping the man with a carefully applied Colt barrel and the hitting with the bottom of the barrel might damage the loading ramrod. Besides that Dusty knew of a far more effective way of silencing a man standing with his back towards him. Balancing lightly on his feet Dusty clenched his fist then struck with his arm held straight. The hard, tight clenched hand smashed right where Tommy Okasi taught him, into the *katsusatsu*, that spot between the fifth and sixth vertebra which could be effectively attacked and with deadly results.

Then sentry stiffened erect. He was all but paralysed by the agony of the unexpected blow and could make no sound. Faster than thought almost Dusty struck again, this time using the *tegatana*, the handsword. The edge of his flat hand smashed into the back of the dazed, rigid man's neck, dropping him to the ground unconscious and without a sound coming from him. Dusty quickly dragged the man round the corner and out of sight then tossed his carbine to one side. Then he went to the door and started to whistle softly, using a tune the other two men knew very well.

Mark Counter and the Ysabel Kid sat on either side of the table in the light of the lantern Bardot had sent to them not so much as a concession of their comfort but as a means of being able to see into the hut through the window. So to all intents the Kid was still fastened, although his hands were free now.

"Bardot won't be round for much longer. He likes his bed too much," Mark said softly. "Then we'll make our move. These French don't take to following orders and still less to doing guards at night. They know the Juaristas move in the darkness."

The Kid grinned back. He too had quite a respect for the Juaristas, or for the Mexicans, as a night fighter. "I'll get by the sentry easy enough and then I'll snake us a couple of hosses from the picket-line. We'll be long gone before they even know what we aim to do."

Mark turned down the light although Bardot had ordered him to keep it on all night. He winked at the Kid and settled down on the bed from which he'd taken all the bedding and substituted it for his own bedroll. They both prepared for a long and trying wait and they got it. On towards midnight they both heard a sound outside the jacal, then a softly whistled tune they both knew. The Kid slid from his chair, catching the Dragoon gun Mark tossed to him and darted on silent feet to the door. That was a friend out there, no other would be whistling "Dixie" to warn them of his pacific intentions.

"Lon, you in there?" a soft voice asked.

"You expecting maybe Robert E. Lee?" the Kid replied as he pulled open the door. "Come in!"

Dusty came in fast, all the faster for he'd seen certain things in the street which told him there was no time for delay. He was no sooner inside than the Kid shut the door behind him. "That ole Nigger hoss of mine—?" he began.

"Get down and make like you're asleep," Dusty cut in through the friendly greeting, his voice showing how serious he thought the situation was. "We're going to have us some callers."

Mark and the Kid obeyed without question although when he came to think about it Mark wondered how Dusty Fog knew he was a friend. However he obeyed, getting on to the bed and laying as if asleep. The Kid sat hunched in his chair and Dusty flattened himself against the wall under the window. This place was well chosen for Mark saw a face at the window, looking in at them. Dusty wondered what the men out there made of the sentry being missing, not knowing that Sergeant Lefarge had given the man orders to clear off shortly before midnight.

Time dragged by and the door of the jacal slowly started to open. Then the big sergeant leant in, his Lefauchex revolver lining on the bed. Mark flung himself off his bedroll, hitting the floor and reaching for his gun. He saw the Kid and Dusty both bringing their guns up and marvelled at the speed of the small man.

Lefarge fired one shot, the bullet making a hole in Mark's prized pillow, a thing he would never travel without. Then Lefarge saw a small figure lunging up from the wall under the window. Even as his shot put out the small light of the lamp he saw the small man's gun swinging up and a blackness came down on the hut, flame tore from the muzzle of the gun. It was the last thing Lefarge saw in this world for Dusty Fog could aim by instinct and memory and the man did not have time to move.

Dusty's guns roared once; the French sergeant reeled backwards into the wall. Even as he fell a second man leapt in showing the futility of standing against an open door when contemplating aggressive action against three skilled pistol shots who were inside and hidden by the darkness. Three guns roared in the dark as Dusty, Mark and the Ysabel Kid fired at the same time. The Frenchman was literally torn to dollrags by the three heavy bullets which picked him up and threw him lifeless through the door to fall on and send blood gushing over Bardot's boots as the officer came to investigate the noise. He'd suspected Lefarge meant to get rid of Mark Counter and allowed his sergeant to carry on for he was sure the man was not only a bully and trouble causer, but also he was watching his officer to report anything to their Colonel. Bardot was a member of the *ancien regime*, his ancestors having escaped the kiss of Madame Guillotine by getting out of France in time. Colonel Mornec, like Lefarge, was of the new order and Lefarge might have received promotion to officer rank if Bardot had not been sent to the regiment by Maximillian. There was little love lost between the elegant aristocrat and the uncouth Colonel. If Lefarge died Bardot would feel better and the killing of Lieutenant Counter would give him a reason to shoot Lefarge.

"What's happening?" he snapped at two men who cowered in front of the jacal. "Get in and see!"

"Sergeant Lefarge is inside," one replied licking his lips and staring at the open door. "I think he is dead."

A bullet from inside the hut narrowly missed Bardot, causing him to duck back to safety. He saw his men pouring from the houses where they'd been resting and coming towards him at a run. "Surround this place!" he yelled. "The American is a traitor and has killed Sergeant Lefarge."

At any other time this news would have been greeted with cheers for Lefarge in common with most sergeants in the French army was hated as a petty tyrant. Now the men fanned into some kind of fighting line and swarmed forward. Two of them went down as the guns in that jacal spat out. The side window broke and a long-barrelled Colt sounded loud, dropping a man with a bullet-smashed shoulder as he ran by.

Bardot saw a regrettable but understandable reluctance amongst his men to take any more risks. He ordered them to shoot at the hut and hold the defenders down, then turned to his corporal and snapped, "Get a torch. We will burn them out."

The corporal hurried away to collect a piece of wood that he could make a torch with. He realised that the man who tried to get close enough to the jacal to throw the torch would have an unenviable task. Running out into the street with a burning piece of wood in the hand would give those straight shooting Americans something of a target which was well within their capabilities.

Bardot watched the man coming back and read something of the reluctance and worry in the way he carried the burning piece of wood. The corporal was worrying for nothing. The first man to try and throw that burning brand on to the jacal would be one of Lefarge's friends. There was no point in leaving any of the Lefarge crowd alive if it could be helped.

"Becque, take the torch and throw it!"

The corporal heard the words with relief for his name was not Becque. He put one hand on the butt of his Lefauchex revolver ready to back up the order with force as he passed the burning piece of wood to Trooper Becque's reluctant hand.

"Give him covering fire," Bardot went on, drawing his revolver. All things must be in order, and the colonel must hear that Bardot acted with military wisdom when they returned with the sad news that Trooper Becque died trying to avenge his sergeant. "Go!"

Becque started forwards, blazing brand in his hand, not knowing that if the Americans in the hut did not kill him Bardot meant to in the confusion. He ran out into the centre of the street while his companions poured shots into the jacal sides and through the open door. He stopped and drew back his arm, the flames licking up hungrily from the wood.

A shot thundered from along the street and Trooper Becque met his end not at the hands of the Americans nor his own officer. The town was suddenly swarming with fast moving Mexicans, advancing and firing as they came. The moon was up now and in its silvery light the men fought with savage skill.

The three Texans stayed in the darkness of the jacal, knowing better than go out into the open and blunder into the fight which was going on outside in the half light. They would be fighting both sides for neither French nor Juarista would speak before shooting.

The Ysabel Kid kicked the door shut, then went to the window and looked out. He could see little for the window looked out over a space between two buildings and there was nothing but shadows. He saw a man dart across the open end of the street. What he saw worried him, for the man wasn't wearing a uniform, and that meant he was a *guerrillo*.

The shots died away and men gathered outside the jacal. From their voices the Kid knew the Mexicans had won this savage night attack and were in full control of the town.

"Come out friends," a voice called.

The Kid felt relieved. His friends understood what was said. That voice had the cultured accent of a Creole, a Spanish born Mexican. "Who is it speaks?" he called back.

"Don Ruis Almonte," the voice came back. "Who are you?"

The Kid felt relieved now and knew there was little danger for this was an old friend of the Ysabel family and although his men were *guerillos* they were loyal Juaristas who fought with no other aim than to win freedom for their country. He knew he could answer up in safety.

"*El Cabrito*," he answered. "With two friends."

"Come out, my young friend."

The Kid stepped out, knowing that the vaqueros who rode for Almonte knew him of old. He saw from their friendly grins that they not only knew, but recognised him. The grins started to fade as Dusty came out for the vaqueros had little time for Tejanos in general. They were wiped off and hard grim lines took their place when Mark came out and they recognised the uniform he wore.

"What is this, *Cabrito*?" tall, lean and elegantly dressed Don Ruis Almonte asked grimly as he looked at the handsome blonde man in the Confederate uniform. "Is he your prisoner?"

"He is my friend. If it was not for him I would be dead now."

"Kill the Americano!" a man yelled, moving forward.

Faster than either Dusty or Mark could move the Ysabel Kid was in front of his friend, the moonlight glinting on the blade of his bowie knife. "Who'll be the first to try?" he asked.

"Put up your knife!" Almonte barked. "Pedro, back! *Cabrito* this man is an enemy and—"

"And I am your friend. I apologise for reminding you but I allowed the men who killed my father to escape while I came to warn you of their plans."

Almonte's face softened. He looked ashamed and inclined his head. "It is I who should apologise for needing reminding. If he is your friend then he will be unharmed by my men."

The Kid's knife went back into leather and he relaxed for he knew that none of the men who rode under Almonte would disobey their leader and patron in any matter. He stepped forward and took Almonte's hand, then introduced Dusty and Mark. After that he explained why he was here and when he mentioned the rifles Almonte nodded. "I've heard of them. They will be of great help to us. I will give you an escort to Monterrey. We took it last week and there are no French there. I am not sure where Benito is and I have not enough money to pay for so many weapons but the commander of the garrison will be able to do so."

It was Dusty who explained why he was here in Mexico. Almonte sat back and listened without a word. At the end Dusty asked, "What do you think?"

"I think Benito will agree. He is a good man and a just one. We would rather fight the entire French army than those wild devils who ride under General Sheldon. Do we pull out tonight?''

Dusty shook his head. During the time in the hut he'd heard about the first of Sam Ysabel's murderers coming here and knew the Kid wanted to stay. He also knew that if he said the word the Kid would leave Giss until some other time.

''We stay. Tomorrow Giss will be coming here and I think Lon wants to meet him.''

''I think he does,'' Almonte agreed.

CHAPTER TEN

Rifle Duel

JOE GISS wasn't a nice man morally or physically. He was tall, lean and cadeverous, with a thin, hard face half hidden by a growth of beard and eyes as hard cold and unfeeling as the eyes of a diamond-back rattler. Along the Rio Grande he was known as a bad man to cross, very unlucky to argue with. He was thoroughly disliked from Pasear Hennessey's outlaw hideout in the west to the eastern coast. The dislike was usually well hidden for Giss was better than fair with a rifle and no mean hand with a Colt gun and not particularly worried about giving the other man an even break.

Yet for all that Giss rode with fear these days and his ordinary wolf caution was increased with the knowledge that his life was in danger. Giss did not fear ghosts and the faces of his murdered victims never troubled him but he was haunted by the ghost of a black-dressed young man who rode a huge white stallion. The fear of the Ysabel Kid grew with each day. Giss and Kraus had sent eight of their best men after the Kid but as the days passed Giss knew they had not succeeded. He regretted having shot down Sam Ysabel and leaving the Kid to his parnter. Kraus was a top-hand with a knife but only a mediocre performer with a rifle. It could not be helped, with a single-shot rifle Giss could not make enough time to drop both Sam Ysabel and his son. Giss scowled down at the butt of the Henry rifle looted from a hacienda after joining the French. With that weapon he could

111

have downed both the Ysabels.

He twisted in the saddle of the French cavalry horse and looked at the patrol riding behind him as they rode slowly along the Santa Juanita trail. Then he turned and looked down at the deserted streets of the town and felt uneasy. He knew a French patrol was there and they had orders to stay out of sight until a stronger relief force joined them but he also knew the poor discipline of the French army when away from their main body. There should have been some signs of the French army and yet there was not.

All his life Giss had been wary and wolf-cautious, his very mode of making a living demanding such caution. In fact, to have lived through thirty-five years of double-dealing and worse showed that his caution paid dividends. So he was constantly on the alert for ambush or trap and some inborn instinct warned him all was not well in Santa Juanita. Yet for all that he did not pass on his fears to the French officer who rode by his side. That was not Giss's way.

"My girth's come loose," he growled.

The French major glanced down and grunted unsympathetically. He did not like Giss's attitude or the easy familarity of the American. However, he was dependent on the scouting ability and on Giss's knowledge of the country so accepted the man's assumption of equality.

Giss halted the horse and then swung down to make the imaginary adjustment to his girth. He allowed the men to ride by him and then as the last one went by swung back into the saddle and followed them.

Carefully Giss scanned the range all round, probing every piece of cover that might conceal a man. Even the lookout rock, which they were now passing, came in for careful scrutiny but Giss could see no sign of anything that might be a *guerillos* ambush.

It would have been the correct thing to tell the Major, then scout the country with more caution but Giss did not mean to do that. There were few worse fates could befall a man than to be taken alive by the *guerillos*. Giss and Kraus might be playing a double game, working for both sides, but the *guerillos* would not know that. Even knowing they might not stay their hands.

Giss's fears were well-founded. In the town of Santa Juanita, Dusty Fog had been very busy. Every sight of the French troops was removed, every sign of the fight in the darkness cleared from the streets. The Mexican *guerillos* were hidden in the jacals and under orders not to fire until the French were right into town. Don Ruis Almonte saw that Dusty was a soldier and a fighting man *par excellence*, one who knew just what he was doing and so let the young Texan lay out the ambush, put the men in their places and give them orders.

The men were now split into small groups and every jacal's open door would soon be pouring death into the French patrol, every shadowy interior bristling with guns. It was war to the death with neither side asking for or giving any quarter. The French would kill all of them if given the same chance and so the ambush was laid to kill the French.

"Reckon they'll obey, Lon?" Dusty asked.

The Ysabel Kid had hardly spoken since the preparations for the ambush were laid out. He stood in the jacal half way along the street with Dusty, Mark and Almonte.

"They'll obey," he finally replied and stood back looking towards the party riding down towards the town.

Yet for all that the Ysabel Kid was worried. Not at Dusty's planning, he had too much faith in the small Texan for that, but he knew the *vaqueros* better than Dusty. They were loyal and obedient to Almonte, but they might not be able to hold down their hatred of the French, the men who despoiled and plundered their country. That was what Dusty was not allowing for. The young *vaqueros* might not be able to hold down their hatred for the French and snap the trap closed too early. Again the Kid did not underestimate the caution Giss would show. The man would be alert for danger and the Ysabel Kid was the first to admit that not even he could show Giss any pointers at smelling out an ambush.

With this in mind the Ysabel Kid had made his preparations for the forthcoming fight. His old Dragoon gun was full-loaded and holstered ready. Sixteen .44 calibre bullets were in the magazine tube of the Henry and one more in the breech ready for action. Another box of bullets bulged his hip pocket ready for use if needed. Further along the street, in an empty jacal, saddled and ready to obey the Kid's signals stood his huge white stallion. If Giss got away this time it would be because the Ysabel Kid was dead.

The French patrol was coming nearer. The watching men saw Giss leave the front of the party and allow the others to ride by him.

"Just like ole Giss," the Kid said, a mirthless grin on his lips, "He smells trouble and he's pulling back. He's got some Injun blood in him, allus thought he had."

"Surely hope these boys remember what you've told them, Dusty," Mark put in.

"So do I," Dusty agreed.

Almonte was silent. He also hoped his men would not forget what they were told but he, like the Kid, knew his men. One of them might forget and spoil the trap. If that happened and Giss got away Almonte would never forgive the man for it would mean his good friend Sam Ysabel would stay unavenged.

The Kid looked round at the others, his face expressionless and his voice low as he said. "Remember, Giss is mine. No matter how it goes it's between me and him."

The French were now riding into town. Even the Major, a man not susceptible to instincts, was realising all was not well. He knew the orders Bardot was given and thought the Captain was holding his men out of sight in proof of the rigid discipline he imposed upon them. Looking along the deserted street, the Major was on the point of halting his troop until a more careful reconnaissance brought some proof that Bardot was here. Before he could give the order he got his proof.

Dusty's ambush was well laid, as well as three years of army experience could lay it. The patrol were riding into the killing area and would be caught in a murderous cross-fire from which there could be no escape. It was unfortunate that there was a new recruit to Almonte's *guerillos*. The other men were old hands at fighting the French and had come as near as any Latin ever could regarding enemies just as someone to fight. That was where Dusty made his mistake. He was used to Anglo-Saxon men who would fight an enemy but still regard him as just another man.

The new recruit was a tall young *vaquero* still in his teens. It was unfortunate that he was in one of the first huts of the town for as he watched the blue-coated soldiers riding by he felt hatred welling up in him. Only a few weeks before such men as these descended on his home, killed his father, raped the women of the house and burned his home to the ground. So he crouched there in the hut watching the hated French riding by and he realised that he had the means for revenge in his hand. Hatred swelled in him and the Dragoon Colt weighed heavily in his hand. He looked at the other men and at last could hold his hatred no longer.

None of the other men in the jacal realised what he was going to do or they would have stopped him. They were at the far side of the hut, in the darkness and waiting for the signal.

"Death to the French."

The young man screamed the words out and hurled from the hut, his old gun roaring out as he landed in the street. He saw one man going down out of his saddle and brought the gun round again.

Dusty saw the young Mexican come from hiding and knew that his carefully made ambush was spoiled. True the bulk of the patrol were in the killing area but Giss, the one man he wanted, was not in it. He also saw the French were seasoned veterans and they would take some handling. The young Mexican only got off one shot before one of the troopers had whirled his horse round and cut the young Mexican down.

Dusty left the jacal in a smooth leap, his bone-handled guns out, even as he sent the French major rolling in the dirt he saw the *guerillos* pouring out from their hiding places. Then the stillness was shattered as French and Mexicans fought in the streets of Santa Juanita.

Dusty, Mark and the Kid were in the street together, guns

out and firing. Even in that wild mêlée as the French charged
at them with drawn sabres Dusty saw that Mark was able to
use a gun with either hand. A cavalryman bore down at them
but five revolvers roared at the same moment and the man
was almost torn to pieces by the heavy lead balls.

It was then the Kid saw Giss turn and run. The Kid was
neither amazed nor surprised at this. The only thing which
surprised him was that Giss had not lit out at the first shot.
Giss whirled his bay gelding and headed back in the direction
he'd come.

Loud over the roar of shots, screams of wounded horses
and shouts of fighting men rang a wild, shattering whistle.
From the jacal where it had stood so patiently came the
Ysabel Kid's big white stallion, racing towards its master like
the devil after a yearling. Without a word to his two friends as
to what he planned the Kid went into action. He thrust the
Dragoon gun back into its holster and with his rifle in his left
hand went afork that seventeen-hand stallion like a bird
flitting into a bush.

Gripping the saddle between his knees the Kid caught up
the loose tied reins and booted the rifle in one move. Then he
was into the French soldiers. He saw a tanned face and the
flash of a lifted sabre and twisted in his saddle, his old
Dragoon coming clear and roaring again, throwing the soft,
round lead ball into the man's chest.

Right into the hail of lead, through the French he rode,
ignoring both *guerillos* bullets and French sabres. His face
was a wild, savage Comanche mask of hatred and his attention given fully to Giss. He fired the old Dragoon without
conscious thought but fighting instinct warned him when the
gun was empty. He saw a French soldier alongside and went
over the side of his saddle as the man swung up his sabre. The
soldier's sabre came down on to an empty saddle where an
instant before was a hard-riding man. The Kid was hanging
over the flank of the horse, riding Comanche style.

Along the street Dusty and Mark both saw the danger the
Kid was in. Dusty twisted sideways and adopted a target
shooting stance, right arm raised, left on his hip. Carefully he

aligned the V-notch in the hammer with the low foresight allowing for the slight low-left bias of the gun fired. He saw the trooper rear up and go sliding over the side of the horse, then saw his own danger, saw it even as he was knocked to one side.

The French major was on his knees, a gun out and lifting at Dusty. The young Texan was so set on saving his friend that he gave the man no attention. But even as Dusty fired Mark saw the danger. The big man's shoulder came down and rammed into Dusty knocking him aside. At the same moment Mark's right-hand gun crashed out, just an instant before the Frenchman's. That instant was enough. The shocking power of the .44 ball striking the major knocked the Lefauchex off aim. Mark felt as if someone had run a hot iron along his arm and knew the bullet had grazed him. He also saw that the French officer had gone over backwards and knew no further bullet was needed.

Then the mad dogfight in the street was over, the guns silent and the wind blowing away the gunsmoke as the last echoes of the shots died away. The street was silent and still again as the *guerillos* looked down at the still, blue clad forms which lay with ever widening pools of blood forming round them. It was over and another savage, bloody battle in Mexico's struggle for freedom had gone to the *guerillos*, though it had been paid for, not all those still shapes were French.

"That was a fool trick, amigo," Dusty remarked as he watched Mark strip off his jacket.

"Sure, I see it now," Mark replied as he rolled back his shirt sleeve and looked at the raw, bloody furrow in the powerful bicep. The bullet had only barely grazed him, the wound was neither deep nor dangerous. "You owe me for a new jacket."

"I'll pay you when we get north again," Dusty answered, then turned to Almonte who came up. "Are there many casualties, señor?"

"Few. We took no prisoners."

Knowing the way the *guerillos* had with prisoners, Dusty

agreed this was for the best. He watched without emotion three wounded French despatched by the Mexican; he'd seen Indians killed the same way. Then he looked back at Almonte who called his men together.

"We will join your friends, Captain," the old Mexican said politely.

Dusty looked out along the trail after the Ysabel Kid and shook his head. "A few more minutes won't make any difference."

Giss rode up the trail from Santa Juanita at a gallop, but at first he was not worried. The French would hold the *guerillos* off his back for long enough to allow him to get away. Then he glanced back and saw a rider coming after him, a man on a big white horse.

Cold fear hit Giss at that moment. He slammed the spurs into his gelding and felt the quiver of response as the horse increased speed. Fast though the big gelding ran it was not fast enough for Giss for he was riding with the fear of death on him. That casual glance back had shown Giss that what he'd feared for the past few weeks was true. There might be other white horses in the West but there were few as big as the Ysabel Kid's Nigger. There were other men in the West who wore all black clothing, too, but the combination of the white stallion and the black dress was enough to tell Giss that the Ysabel Kid was after him.

Even as he twisted in his saddle for another look Giss saw the white was closing on his gelding and knew that he could not outrun the Ysabel Kid. All too well he knew how that white could both run and stay at speed. He also knew the Kid would cling to his trail now and it was many miles before Giss could hope to find another French patrol. Long before he could get there Giss knew the Kid would catch up with him.

With this in mind, the Ysabel Kid coming along fast and no chance to escape, Giss knew he must fight. Then he grinned savagely as he thought of the Henry rifle in his saddleboot. It was full loaded with fifteen bullets and could fire far more rapidly than the Ysabel Kid's old Hawken which needed reloading after each shot. Then Giss remembered, Kraus's bullets smashed the Hawken on the day he, Giss, killed Sam Ysabel. Unless the Kid had got hold of another rifle he would be left with that carbine stocked Dragoon, not a long range weapon, and one the Henry could outrange. Even if the Kid did own a new rifle he would not have found time to get practice in long range work with it.

Lookout Rock loomed ahead and Giss knew that here was where he must make his stand. There was little cover for the Kid, and none Giss couldn't sight on from the top of the rock. All he had to do was get behind the rock and wait to see what weapon the Kid used, then when the Kid's gun was empty get to the top of the rock and take careful aim. It was a real pity about the eight men they'd sent after the Kid. They were good men, but not good enough it seemed.

Giss hurled down from his horse, sliding the rifle from his saddleboot as he went, and allowing the horse to go free he ducked behind the rock. The gelding came to a halt, the hanging reins stopping it from wandering far. Giss brought up his Henry and lined it on an empty saddle. The white was wheeling off to one side but the Ysabel Kid was no longer riding it. A bullet slapped into the rock sending chips into Giss's face and causing a very rapid draw back into cover.

The Ysabel Kid knew Giss very well, knew him and guessed how he was thinking. The man was running but knew too well that he could not escape the big white stallion. So Giss would pick his place for the fight and there would be no better place than there at the Lookout Rock. There Giss would fort up, relying on the extra range of his rifle to bring him through.

It was just before he dived from the saddle that the Kid saw what kind of weapon Giss was now carrying. A wolf-savage grin split the Kid's face as he jerked the rifle from his saddleboot and went from leather to the shelter of a small rock. So ole Giss had got hold of a Henry rifle. Good. That evened things a mite.

The Kid lit down and went into the shelter of the rock in one move even as Giss left his own horse. They were separated by a distance of about sixty yards, these two men. The Kid's yelled order sent his white stallion racing off in a half circle to halt out of range and shot, there to wait for whatever order came next.

The Kid's rifle cracked out once.

Only one thing saved Giss. The Ysabel Kid had not yet managed to do much long range shooting with his new rifle. Sixty or more yards was a long range with the rimfire cartridge of the 44/28 Henry rifle. Due to the comparatively weak base, necessary with rimfire, percussion could not hold the forty-grain charge of the later centre-fire models. Even so he saw the rock chips kick up near Giss's head and was satisfied. With his old Hawken he would have sent the ball through Giss's head, but he knew the old weapon's vagaries. It wasn't bad shooting with a new rifle, not over that range. Now all he needed to do was experiment until he knew how the range would affect the bullets. After that it would be all over for Giss.

At the shot Giss, expecting the Kid to be busy with powder flask, patch, ball and ramrod, came out of cover. His rifle lined and fired and as an echo to the shot a bullet tore his hat from his head and caused him to make a rapid dive for cover again. He flattened against the wall of the rock and sweat ran down his face. It was a moment or so before he could steady his nerves and he licked his lips as he realised the Ysabel Kid had a repeater down there. From the sound of the shot it was a Henry .44 rifle, not the deep-throated bellow of the carbine stocked Dragoon Colt. Nor did it have the deeper bellow of the .56 calibre Spencer. That meant the Kid owned a Henry now. However the Kid had fired two shots, Giss figured as his nerves settled again. That left him, if his magazine was full to start with, thirteen more bullets. Giss had only fired one shot leaving him with fourteen bullets, one up on the Kid and at the end of the Kid's magazine load he would have the great advantage that one bullet gave.

Laying behind the rock where he'd dived the Ysabel Kid regarded his habitation with some disfavour. It gave him just enough cover to be safe and was neither comfortable nor shady, but the Kid was Comanche enough to disregard personal comfort at such a time. He concentrated, not on hitting the difficult target Giss gave him but on ranging in the rifle. Already he was seeing what Dusty had known all along, that the repeating qualities of the Henry were gained at the expense of range.

Giss appeared briefly and fired, the bullet ricocheting into the air and the Kid fired back, watching the strike of his bullet against the rock. The rifle held fairly true even at that range, yet not true enough for him to rely on it. In six months' time, when he'd made more practice with the rifle the Kid would be able to call his shots with his original uncanny accuracy, but at the moment he was still getting the feel of the weapon.

Again Giss fired and the Kid shot back at him. Giss grinned, noting the way the bullets were hitting and knowing that he was safe for the time being unless he gave the Kid too easy a mark. He was still one shot behind the Kid.

"What happened to Sanchez and his men?"

"Dead, all of them. I got three before I left Mexico, and the others over the Texas line," the Kid yelled back. "You never could pick good men."

"So you come back down here after me!"

"You 'n' Kraus both. Where's he at?"

"With the Mexicans some place. We're playing both sides. If the French win ole Kraus comes over and I say he's been working for them. If the greasers win he does the same for me."

"Figgered it. We got Charro!"

Giss grunted. Charro had been his right hand man and sent on a mission to Kraus. If the Kid knew what Charro had been carrying he would have been some surprised.

"I'll tell Kraus when I meet him."

"That'll be in hell!"

Giss rocked into view and fired a fast shot which sent splinters into the air just over the Kid's head, then fired again as the Kid came up to answer. His bullet missed the dark boy by inches and the Kid fired three times as fast as he could work the lever and pull the trigger. The bullets caused Giss to flatten back against the rock but he was satisfied for the Kid was two shots behind him.

Firing again Giss jerked back, but this time he did not draw a shot in return. He moved around the base of the rock and looked cautiously out. It took him a couple of moments to locate where the Kid was hiding for Indian smart, he was not allowing himself to be seen any more than possible. All Giss could see was the top of the Kid's boot but he lined on that. If the bullet hit near enough it might make the Kid rear up into view for he was watching the other side of the rock and might panic. It was a chance and Giss took it.

The Kid was all too aware of his danger and he also was counting the shots for he knew what was going on in Giss's mind all the time. Knew it and took savage Comanche pleasure in the shock the other man would get. Then the Kid himself got a shock. The shot came from the other side of the rock and a bullet ripped into the ground just behind his foot. Yet for all of that the Kid's nerves were under such control that he neither jumped out of his place nor panicked in any way. With a rolling twist he was round the side of the rock away from Giss and came up to fire back; there was a rapid exchange of shots, but neither hit. Now the Kid had seven bullets left, according to Giss's calculations while he himself still held eight.

Giss ducked back again and lay on the ground, studying the rock behind which the Kid lay. Then his eyes went to the side of Lookout Rock facing the Kid. This side was a far gentler slope than the others and a set of steps had been carved out on this slope by the villagers allowing for rapid ascent or descent from the top. When the Kid's rifle was empty Giss would dash up those steps and on top would be able to see the Kid and also take an easy shot. He knew he would be safe from his own experience of the Henry rifle for, despite the manufacturer's boasts it took time to draw the magazine spring to the muzzle end, open the magazine tube, insert bullets then shut the tube and slide back the spring. It took seconds and the Ysabel Kid would not have the seconds to spare, or if he had Giss would be very surprised.

"I should have dropped you instead of your ole man, Kid!" Giss yelled, trying to annoy the Kid and make him do something foolish.

"You should." The Kid was not going to be provoked. His red hazel eyes were cold as he lined the rifle again. He was already getting to know how the rifle shot and how each current of moving air affected the bullet over a range. "It was the worst day's work you ever did when you dropped him."

"He should have joined us then we wouldn't. Both sides are paying us."

"You'll never live to spend it."

Giss fired and every time he shot an answering spurt of flame came from the small rock. Giss was getting worried now for he noted that the Kid's bullets were starting to hit the same spot on the rock every time. Eight, nine, ten, eleven, twelve shots Giss counted from the Kid's rifle, leaving him with only two bullets. Yet for all that Giss knew his danger. The Kid was getting to know his rifle now and would be able to call his shots. Giss fired again, the answering bullet narrowly missed his face and screamed into the air causing him to jerk himself back into cover again. It took some moments before Giss could raise enough courage to try and draw the last shot.

With the crack of the Kid's rifle Giss came from behind the rock and raced for the steps, climbing wildly up. At the top he turned, breathing hard and looked down. The Ysabel Kid was kneeling in plain view, his rifle lining up. Giss grinned as he saw the Kid, unused to repeating rifles, had not counted his shots. With fifteen bullets gone from his rifle the black dressed boy was at Giss's mercy and would soon meet the same end as his father. Giss lined the rifle, the sights making a perfect picture on the centre of the Kid's shirt. Then Giss waited for the Kid to squeeze the trigger of his rifle and hear the hollow click which would tell him the weapon was empty and of no use.

That was where Giss made his mistake. The Henry he

carried and that he'd looted from a hacienda to the south took only fifteen bullets. The rifle the Kid held was not an old model. It was one of the new pattern, a pattern Giss had never seen. It was a far superior weapon to the old Henry and among its innovations it held not fifteen but seventeen shots.

Flame tore from the barrel of the Ysabel Kid's rifle. Giss felt the sudden, shocking impact as lead struck him. He reared up and through the whirling pain haze saw the Kid get up, take out a bullet and push it towards the breechplate of the rifle. Then the Kid lifted his weapon again, his right eye sighted along the smooth blue barrel and his finger squeezed the trigger lovingly. Even though Giss was staggering, the Ysabel shot and hit. Giss rocked back on his heels, threw his rifle to one side and crumpled forward. He lay there on top of the Lookout Rock dead without ever finding out how he came to make the mistake which cost him his life.

The Ysabel Kid shoved more bullets through the loading gate of his rifle, then crossed the open ground fast. He held the rifle ready for instant use and never took his eyes off the still form on top of the big rock. He was very cautious as he climbed the rock, ready to shoot at the first move, but his caution was not needed. Giss lay still, two holes in his body, either of which would have caused his death.

For a time the Kid stood looking down at the body of his father's killer. The dark face showed none of his feelings as he rolled Giss's body over the edge of the rock and let it crash to the ground below.

"I thought you were counting on me being a shot ahead of you. Giss. You never was but half smart."

Climbing down again the Ysabel Kid caught Giss's horse, mounted it and rode away. He did not bother to search Giss for he knew his man. Giss would never be fool enough to carry anything in writing on him. He preferred to make use of his excellent memory and carry a message in his head. There was no danger of losing it then.

The big white stallion moved back to its master, eyeing the other horse aggressively. The Kid reached over and rubbed the white's sleek neck and then kneed the gelding forward. The white followed him along without needing reins or anything to keep it coming. The Kid turned and looked back, his face still cold and hard. The man who killed his father was dead, but there was still one other one to get.

CHAPTER ELEVEN

Dusty Hires Two

DUSTY FOG and Mark Counter stood together watching the Ysabel Kid riding back towards them. They'd been able to see something of the long range duel which was going on out there, but bound by their word to the Kid they made no attempt to interfere.

They walked along the street, ignoring the *guerrillos* who were now preparing food before they travelled on again. Dusty and Mark were hungry but they went to the edge of town to wait and see what the Ysabel Kid had to say.

For a moment none spoke as they met. Then Dusty held out his hand, and gripped the Kid's hard.

"That's one of them, Lon."

"I'll get the other, too," the Kid answered, then noticed that Mark's coat sleeve was torn. "You all right, amigo?"

"Likely live. No fault of yours though."

"Giss carrying any papers, Lon?" Dusty put in.

"Nope, he wouldn't be. You pair all right?"

"All right?" Mark growled angrily. "All right. Since I met up with you two I've had nothing but troubles. I've been shot at by the French, nearly gunned down by the Mexicans, had my pillow torn up, my arm nicked and you say are you all right? I tell you I've never had so much trouble since I left home to join the army."

"Maybe it'll be better next time," the Kid said consolingly.

127

"Sure maybe next time they'll kill you," Dusty went on.

Mark looked at the other two for a moment, then he threw back his head and laughed. He put a big arm around each one's shoulder and they returned along the street to where Don Ruis Almonte waited to serve them with a meal.

Tom Alden was a worried man as he rode with Conway at the head of the large group of mules. He constantly turned his head to look back over the bunch of animals following the bell-mare. He ignored the man leading the mare, the flank riders of the mule train and looked at the distant horizon trying vainly to get some sight of the two Texans who'd helped him so much. It never occurred to him that Dusty Fog or the Ysabel Kid might be dead or that they might get in more trouble than they could handle. In the few short days he'd known Dusty Fog he'd got to think that there was nothing the small man could not do. Even when the Kid's horse returned riderless he was not worried for Dusty had gone out and Alden was sure that Dusty could get the Kid back.

"Soon be too dark to travel any more, Tom," Conway remarked. "Wish the Kid was here. He knows this country."

"You've got your own man out as a scout."

"Sure, but Mick doesn't know this country like the Kid does. He's a fair scout but there's only one Ysabel Kid."

Alden agreed with this. They were making a wide swing round the town of Santa Juanita as a matter of simple precaution. That had been Dusty's orders before he left them. The mule train was kept moving in the general direction of Monterrey and Conway was using his regular scout instead of leaving it to the Ysable Kid.

They made camp on the banks of a stream for the night, holding the mules out in the open. Due to the shortage of men Alden rode his circle on the mules with the other men. There was nothing happening that night and the animals were all too leg weary to try and break away from the bunch.

It was late the following afternoon when Mike came up from one of his wide swings round the mule-train with the disquieting news that a large bunch of men were following them. They were still in the rolling, open country and the men, looking back, could faintly see a large bunch of riders coming after them. There was no way of telling yet who the men were, or even if they were French or Mexican. One thing was for sure those men were travelling faster than the mules could, and would soon catch up.

Alden turned in his saddle and looked back. Those riders were coming closer with every minute and now it was sure they were following the mule-train. They were a deadly danger whoever they were. If it was a French patrol it was large enough to take the muleskinners in a straight fight. The French would be only too pleased to get this consignment of arms, and the thousand Henry repeaters would make a vast difference to their fighting capabilities. There would be no chance of selling the arms either, for the French would kill every man here and take all they wanted. Even if the men following were Mexicans it might not be much better for he knew the *guerillos* might take it into their head to acquire the arms without payment.

"Can we get more speed out of the mules, Mike?" he asked, thinking of the effect on his company the loss of this shipment would mean.

Times were hard for the Winchester Repeating Firearms Company at the moment, with O. F. Winchester's failure to make a big army contract and other expenses piling up. The sale of these rifles down here would make all the difference to the Company being able to carry on or failing through lack of finance.

"No chance," Conway replied. "We've worked them harder than usual now. I was aiming to get a day's rest for them. If we try to work them any faster they'll be dropping on us."

"What do you think we'd best do then?"

"Keep moving and hope they lose us in the dark. If they don't we'll be in bad trouble. Even a bunch of French soldiers could follow the trail we're leaving."

Alden turned again and looked back over the rolling country at that bunch of riders which was slowly drawing nearer.

He hated the steady way they were closing in on him and bringing with them an end to all his plans and hopes. H swore that before he would let these arms fall into the hand of the French he would destroy all of them. His men would each take a rifle and they would fight back. There was more ammunition on the mules than they were ever likely to use and they might be able to hold off the men who were follow ing them.

Mick, the scout, came racing back and brought his horse to a rearing, sliding halt. He looked excited and waved a hand ahead of them.

"There's a deep basin about half a mile ahead. If we can get in there they'll have the devil's own time getting us ou again."

Conway and Alden put petmakers to their horses and li out after the scout. They rode up to the edge of the basin and saw that it answered all their prayers. Whatever had caused this depression in the ground they did not know. It was abou half a mile square with gently sloping, rock covered slopes leading down to the smooth, rich grass of the bottom. It was just what they needed for a fort up and they would be the first men to follow the as yet unspoken advice: "When in bad trouble fort up with a Winchester".

"Point 'm down there, me boyos," Mick roared to his men. "We'll stand here and if they want a fight, then we'll give 'em one."

The men yelled their approval for every one of these riders was a hardy Irish fighting man and wanted to try out the potentials of these Henry rifles. The man leading the bell-mare turned and headed for the basin. Slowly the untidy looking bunch of mules turned and straggled after her, down to the bottom of the basin. There they discovered that they were not expected to walk any more and some settled to graze.

Alden stayed with the men only long enough to tell them to break out the rifles and ammunition then dashed back up the slope again. In his hands he held a new model Henry and he flipped open the lever as he landed behind the rock he'd chosen for his fighting position. He looked as the riders came gradually nearer, squinting his eyes and trying to see who they were. At that distance he still was unable to tell much about the riders.

"Looks bad, Tom," Conway slid down beside him holding a Hawken muzzle loader. "There's a fair bunch of them coming after us."

"Too many?"

"Devil a bit, not for us Irish."

Time dragged by; the steady advance of the riders continued and gradually the worry lines left Conway's face. He recognised the big paint and white horses at the head of the party even before he could distinguish the riders. Then even as Alden's eye picked out the white and the paint Conway was sure that the Ysabel Kid and Dusty Fog were riding towards them at the head of the other men.

It was some time before Conway relieved Alden's worry as to who the riders were, and by that time Alden himself could tell the horses. It said much for the esteem Dusty was held in by the other men that even before they could tell it was he and the Ysabel Kid neither doubted for a moment that Dusty had rescued the Kid.

"Now what the hell's the Cap'n been and done," Conway asked, "and who's that bunch he's got with him?"

Alden shook his head. It was beyond him for although he could see the great part of the approaching group were Mexicans riding alongside Dusty, the Kid and the tall hidalgo at the front of the group was undoubtedly a Confederate army officer. That was a mixture and Alden could not even start to think how they all came to be together or the Confederate officer was not, as might be expected, a prisoner.

Dusty Fog looked down into the basin as he halted his horse and then asked mildly, "Expecting somebody, Tom?"

"What?" Alden growled, the relief he felt bursting in sudden anger at these two grinning young men who'd caused him so much anxiety with so little cause. "Why you—"

"You could have wigwagged us, Dusty," Conway went on in aggrieved tone. "We thought you were the French and after us.''

Dusty looked round at the men who were still in their defensive positions and then down at the mules quietly grazing in the botton of the basin. He turned and looked back over the rolling country and made his decision.

''Tom, if there's any water round get the mules to it. We'll night up down here.''

Alden waited until after Conway went to make the arrangements for watering the mules, then turned back to Dusty and asked, ''What's all this about?''

''Not much at all. This here's Lieutenant Mark Counter of the Sheldon troops and Don Ruis Almonte. Don Ruis will escort us to Monterrey and Mark's going along to meet General Sheldon with us from there.''

There was a lot hidden in those soft spoken words, that Alden was real sure about. How Dusty came to find a Mexican with enough men to give them a safe escort to Monterrey and a Confederate officer to act as guide to Bushrod Sheldon beat Alden.

Almonte's men went to help the muleskinner unload and tend the stock while Dusty and Almonte prepared the defence of the basin. The *guerrillos* were split up into small groups and sent out as flanking pickets all round the hollow where the main party was grouped. Their orders were to watch for any French patrols and if they saw one to let it go by if it was not headed for the basin. If it was they were to try and decoy it away. The rifles must be protected at all costs in Almonte's view and Dusty agreed with it.

Only a skeleton party was to remain in the basin with the muleskinners and to these Dusty gave stringent orders about keeping quiet after dark and not showing any cooking fires at all. Any cooking was to be done now, in the last light of day and every fire was to be out before full darkness.

''We could do with resting up the mules for a day, Dusty.''

It was Conway who came up with the next problem as Dusty stood watching the men taking small groups of animals off to water them.

Dusty watched the animals, noting how leg weary they

were. Mike Conway made his living from these animals and he was worried about them. It was vitally important to get the mules to Monterrey and see the rifles handed over to Juarez but it would be of no use if the mules could not carry the weight. Like every army commander Dusty was aware that not only a day but minutes could make the difference in a war. He had to balance the risk of the mules foundering against the extra day of rest.

"All right, Mike, take your day. Don Almonte, we'll camp here for one day then move on."

Almonte nodded his approval. This small man in the dress of a cowhand was a soldier through and through. It pleased the old Don that Dusty had taken the full responsibility without hesitation for he would have liked to offer his opinion on the matter. Like Dusty, Almonte knew that Conway depended for his living on the mules and was willing to allow them a one day respite for the travelling they had been forced into.

To the muleskinners it came as a well-earned break from the trail and they were prepared to enjoy it. With the usual cheerful Irish way they made friends with the *guerrillos* or renewed old friendships, for Conway's men had delivered more than one contraband cargo to Almonte's hacienda. They made their meals around the small fires then as night came down doused each blaze. The night was warm and as the moon came up there was no need for a fire to help them see their way about.

After making sure all was as he wanted it, Dusty came back to join Mark and the Ysabel Kid. He made a tour of the pickets and found the men, much to his surprise, alert and watchful. Now he settled down on his bedroll and looked at the bulk of Mark Counter next to him.

"What're you fixing to do when we've finished down here, Mark?"

For a time Mark did not reply. He was tired of army life and knew that he was too independent ever to make a success-ful career officer. Also he had no intention of ever wearing a Union army uniform even though one of the concessions to be made to Sheldon was that any man who wished could join the Union army with his present rank and seniority. There was his father's big R over C spread down in the Big Bend country but it was in the very capable hands of Rance Counter and Mark's three older brothers. There was work for him there but he knew the others could manage equally well without him. He was willing to listen to any suggestion Dusty might make.

"Reckon I'll look round for a riding chore."

"Uncle Devil wants me to get men for his floating outfit. I'm going to run it and I'd be real pleased if you'll take on as my segundo."

Mark grinned at Dusty, his firm white teeth gleaming against the tan of his face. A floating outfit was almost a mobile ranch. Five or six men who spent all their time away from the main outfit, out on the far parts of the spread's range, doing the same kind of work the other ranch hands did closer in. With Dusty in command it promised to be a very stimulating and enterprising group.

"I'm on," Mark replied, then looking at the Ysabel Kid. "Are you in this, too, Lon?"

Now it was the Kid's turn to think. He'd been expecting this sort of invitation from the start and thinking over what he should say. Then his face also split in a wide grin. Those two hell twisters would do to ride the river with. He found that the idea of running contraband and following the smuggler profession was no longer attractive, not when one could ride with two good friends like these pair.

"Tell you, if you'll promise I don't have to meet too many sheriffs or go near too many jails I reckon I could give it a whirl."

Dusty was satisfied. Ole Devil's ideas of the floating outfit was not only for the purpose of handling the range work away from the ranch house. He also wanted a capable fighting force on hand to help out any of his friends who found themselves in trouble. With Mark Counter and the Ysabel Kid on call, Dusty was sure he had the nucleus of that fighting force and his cousin Red Blaze, would form the fourth member of the group if needed.

"Likely Uncle Devil'll fire me when he sees what I've straddled him with but I'll take a chance on it. You're hired."

"When's payday?" the Ysabel Kid inquired.

"Pity we can't move in tomorrow," Mark put in.

"It's only one more day," Dusty answered.

Mark groaned. He loved his comfort and never believed in sleeping out when he might be in a bed. Now he was condemned to two nights out in the open when he'd hoped to find a comfortable resting place in Monterrey on the following night. Not only that but far worse, he was compelled to use his saddle for a pillow as the Lefauchex bullet had torn his pillow beyond any hope of repair.

The night was silent enough now and the moon up, lighting the bottom of the basin almost as if it was day. The men were almost all in their bedrolls, or just laying on the ground. Dusty lay there relaxed and studying the Ysabel Kid who was sleeping next to him. The Kid's many talents would find full use in the floating outfit and he would be steered clear of the outlaw trails he was used to riding.

The Kid came awake, and sat up, hand going to the old Dragoon. Dusty watched, noting that complete change from sleep to full awake which told a man who was long used to danger.

"What is it, Lon?" he asked.

"Somebody's coming in," the Kid's reply was just a whisper.

Dusty was several seconds before he could hear the approaching man, but the Kid was already holstering his gun. They rose and walked through the sleeping camp followed by Mark and Almonte. The men appeared to be asleep and the mules were all bedded down, either asleep or grazing.

The man who'd come out from the night was one of the pickets coming to bring some alarming news. A large French force was moving across country and would be passing the camp area at about half a mile. This would be the testing time; the French patrol might be looking for them, or it might be taking advantage of the darkness to avoid clashing with the Mexican forces. If the French were looking for Alden and his shipment of rifles they would be alert for any sound and would be watching for any sign.

This was the testing time for Dusty's arrangements. If all was silent the French patrol might pass them in the night without even knowing they were there. It was lucky that all the men were asleep—

"Oh the English came and tried to teach us their
    ways,
They scorned us just for being what we are,
But they might as well have tried to catch a moon-
    beam,
Or light a penny candle on a star."

The words of an Irish rebel song were being sung in a drunken tenor voice from the other side of the camp.

Dusty sprang round. He could hear men stirring and knew it was only a matter of seconds before they were talking amongst themselves and asking questions. From then it was only a matter of more seconds before there was so much noise the French would hear it as they passed.

"Quiet!" he snarled to a bunch of men as he passed them, the concentrated savagery in his tone making their voices dry off immediately.

"That you, Cap'n?" it was Mike Conway looming up in the darkness.

"Sure!" Dusty bit down the sarcastic reply which came to his lips. "Who's that making all that noise, Mike?"

"Raffety. He's got a bottle of tequila from one of the vaqueros and he's been at it for a spell now."

"Has he," Dusty refrained from asking why the man was allowed to drink. "We'll have to stop him."

Conway grunted something unintelligible as Dusty went by. Then following the leader of the muleskinners said, "He'll not let you, Cap'n. He ain't a bad man but he gets mean when the likker's in him. When he starts to singing Galway Bay he's bad mean and even I can't do anything with him.''

The Ysabel Kid had disappeared with the picket and came back fast, travelling at a loping run. He brought disquieting news. The French, though still far enough away, were coming in this direction and would pass at much less than the half mile the other man estimated.

Dusty went across the basin fast followed by Mark, the Kid and several other men, to where Raffety sat in solitary state. The man was seated with his back to a large rock, the tequila bottle in his hand and his voice giving out with another verse about how the wicked English downtrod the Irish people. He looked up truculently as Dusty halted in front of him.

For an instant Dusty glared down at the man who despite his tenor voice was almost as tall and quite a bit heavier than Mark. This did not influence Dusty at all and before Mark could start to make the suggestion he handled the matter it was too late. Dusty's hand stabbed out, took the bottle from Raffety's hand and threw it to one side.

If a jackrabbit had walked up and kicked him Raffety could not have been more surprised. He was used to folks giving him a clear trail when drunk and it took him a moment or two to realise that this small man dare come up and throw his bottle away.

With a snarl of anger Raffety came up, hand fanning towards his gun. Dusty moved in, fist driving into Raffety's muscled but tequila-filled belly with all his strength behind the blow. Mark, no mean hand at any branch of barehand fighting looked his approval, noting the way the entire weight of Dusty's body was behind the punch. Hard though it was it did not put Raffety down. It brought a grunt of pain from him and made his hand miss the butt of his gun but that was all.

The big man's hand drove out in a punch that should have knocked Dusty clear across the basin but it missed. The small Texan moved his head aside and the force of the blow threw Raffety forward. The big man felt two hands grip the front of his shirt then Dusty went down, ramming a foot into Raffety's stomach. The big man went forward with his own weight, then his feet left the ground and he sailed over to light down flat on his back. Mumbling curses Raffety rolled on to his hands and knees and came up.

"Give it up, Irish!" Dusty snapped, for his patience was wearing thin and he knew that if Raffety did not stop he was going to get hurt bad.

Raffety, unfortunately was too drunk to see the quiet menace in the determined expression on Dusty's face. He hurled forward again, huge hands clawing out to envelope the small Texan in a murderous bear hug. Mark bit down his yell of warning and was about to leap forward to help his friend when Dusty struck. The Texan's hand moved almost faster than the eye could follow, yet Mark saw that the fist was not held tight clenched in the normal way. The forefinger was so bent that it stood out in advance of the other knuckles. It was this bent finger that landed, right under Raffety's nose. The big man stopped dead, his arms crumpling down to his sides as a look of agony such as Mark had rarely if ever seen before passed over his face. Then without a sound Raffety collapsed to the ground and lay without a move.

"What the hell, Dusty?" Mark asked. "I thought I knew something about fist fighting but I never saw a man put down like that before, or a fist held like—"

"Quiet all of you!" Dusty's voice was the anger filled snarl of a martinet officer. The men who were talking loudly and eagerly about what they'd seen, all fell silent. "I'll explain it later, Mark. Right now ain't such a good time."

The men broke up and headed for the slopes under Dusty's savagely hissed commands like children when an irascible father raises his voice in anger. The broken silence closed down again.

"Watch the French, Lon," Dusty said softly.

The Kid faded into the darkness again and the men grew more silent as they heard the sound of approaching horses and the creak of saddle leather. They had been so engrossed in watching Dusty handle Raffety that they had not noticed the sound of the approaching French. Now they did and most of them cursed the now unconscious Raffety and realised why their unofficial leader took such drastic steps to stop the drunken singing.

The men on the slopes of the basin almost held their breath as the long line of French troops rode by at a distance of about a quarter of a mile. There was many a sigh of relief when the Ysabel Kid, who'd followed the French, came back to report that all was well. The French were riding on, not showing any signs of camping near by.

Dusty watched the other men going back to their bedrolls and then gave a grunt of relief. "That was too close for me."

CHAPTER TWELVE

In Old Monterrey

"HOW did you put Raffety down, Dusty?" Mark inquired as they rode along the last leg of the journey towards Monterrey. "He was unconscious for four hours. I thought you'd killed him."

"I was scared I might have myself," Dusty admitted. "The trouble with using the forefinger fist on the philtrum is if you do it too hard, it can kill the man."

Mark looked back along the line to where Raffety hunched in his saddle, his top lip swollen almost double its normal size.

"I've never seen a man go down like he did and I've hit a few on the nose," Mark objected.

"Sure you hit them on the nose. Just under the nose, right in the centre of the top lip is the place to aim. But an ordinary fist won't do it. You have to get the exact spot and to do that you hold your hand in what Tommy Okasi calls the forefinger fist, like this." Dusty demonstrated the way he'd folded his fist the night before last.

Mark thought this over. He was skilled in all branches of frontier fist fighting and had learned the art of boxing from a professional pugilist friend of his father. However this technique Dusty used was new to him and appeared to be something well out of the ordinary. He felt new respect for his friend; there did not seem to be any end to the talents of Dusty Fog.

The town of Monterrey loomed ahead of them, sprawling out in the heat of the noon-day sun. The French were driven from this area and the fighting was farther south and more towards the coast.

The town was taking its siesta when Dusty Fog brought his party in. The noise of the many horses and mules brought sleepy-eyed men and women from where they carried out the ancient and noble custom of old Mexico. By the time they reached the main square, quite a crowd was gathered, yelling greetings both to the *guerillos* and to the Ysabel Kid who appeared to be well-known and liked here.

In the large, open plaza Dusty raised his hand bringing the mules to halt. He turned to Alden and asked, "Do you reckon we'd better hole up somewhere with the rifles until we're paid?"

"Might be at that," Alden agreed. He for one did not intend allowing the Mexican Army to get hold of the weapons until the money was paid over.

The Ysabel Kid pointed to a large, deserted looking building on the side of the plaza. "We'll take them in there. It belongs to a friend of mine, who is off fighting the French. He won't mind if we use it."

Dusty looked the building over. It was separated from the other establishments by some thirty feet on either side. Then riding forward Dusty entered the building, leaving his paint standing with reins hanging loose. The inside of the building was simple in the extreme. It was just one big room with a scarred wooden bar at one end. There were windows at each side although these had no glass in them. All in all, it would be a good place to fork up. To make sure Dusty went to the rear window and looked out. The nearest buildings was some thirty or more yards away and it was all open ground in between.

After testing the pump behind the bar and finding it worked Dusty went to the door and called, "Unload and bring it in here."

The watching citizens of Monterrey showed great interest in the loads those mules were carrying although their interest was not enough for them to offer help in the unloading. Their help was not needed for the Conway men and the *guerrillos* were more than enough to carry the rifles in and stack them in piles of fifty on the floor. The boxes of ammunition were stacked up also in neat piles and as a precaution Dusty had a couple of them broken open ready for use.

Alden handed one of the presentation rifles to Mark Counter and showed him how to load it. Mark examined the piece with interest, hefting it and testing the balance. "Fine looking rifle," he said to the Kid.

"Best I've ever handled," the Kid replied.

Conway came into the building, going straight to Dusty and from the look on his face he was worried.

"Dusty, I just heard that Chavelinos is in command down here. Don Ruis's just gone to see him."

"So?"

"Chavelinos and me don't get on together," Conway replied, glancing at the Ysabel Kid for confirmation.

"That's right, Dusty," the Kid agreed. "Can't say I like Chavelinos much myself. He was only a captain so how come he's in command?"

"He's a general now. The devil only knows how he got to be one. The Mexican Army can't be that badly off for men," Conway growled. "I reckon me and the boys best pull out; we'll only make trouble for you if we stop here."

The Kid nodded his agreement to this. Chavelinos and Conway had a long standing feud and it might go hard for the muleskinner to be caught in a town where Chavelinos held the power.

Dusty was willing to accept the Kid's word for this and knew that Conway and his men could do little to help them now. He called Alden over and passed on the news. The big salesman did not argue, but made Conway out a bank draft for his services and shook hands.

"Thanks Mike, it's been good knowing you. If you ever need a friend get in touch with the Winchester Repeating Firearms Company and I'll do what I can for you."

"I'll remember that," Conway replied.

Shortly after Conway and his men left the town leading their pack mules and headed back north as fast as they could make it.

"What do you reckon'll happen now, Lon?" Dusty asked as they watched Conway's men leave town.

"I'd take money that Chavelinos tries to get the guns without paying for them."

"We'd best get ready for war then," Dusty looked at the building they were in. It would be a good fort in case of trouble.

Almonte returned soon after, his face troubled as he halted his horse in front of the building and looked down at Dusty.

"I have orders to take my men out again. The money is here and General Chavelinos is under orders to pay for the arms. I'm afraid he will try to get them without payment."

"You mean a double-cross?" Dusty asked.

"By Chavelinos. He would never dare try it if Benito was near."

"What do you aim to do about it?"

"My orders from Chavelinos is to patrol the northwest so I think Benito is to the Southeast. It is in that direction I will lead my men. I will try to get back here before Chavelinos can make any trouble."

Almonte turned and rode out of town at the head of his men. Dusty did not waste any time in futile worrying over what he'd been told. He looked round and saw that this place was ideal for them to fort up in. The walls would stop a ball fired from a Mexican musket and any attempt to cross the open ground would be under the fire of the Henry repeaters. Unless there was some way of stopping the water to the pump they would be all right as far as that went. It was just food for themselves and the horses which would be the problem.

Until they knew definitely that Chavelinos was not going to pay for the weapons there was no need for them to worry unduly. It had been a wise precaution Mark's borrowing a civilian shirt and stowing his uniform jacket out of sight. With Mark in uniform there would be some excuse for Chavelinos showing caution in dealing with them.

Chavelinos was General but not by virtue of his attainments unless the use of unmitigated gall is an attainment. He came into the rank in the very confused days of the early struggle against the French. A mere Quartermaster Branch officer he'd been looked down on by the arrogant Mexican Spanish gentleman officers, products of the Military College of Mexico and despised by the hard ex-bandido officers whose career of outlawry attracted such attention that they were given a commission in the Army to reduce the costs they were incurring.

His rise to the rank of General was fast though hardly official. Calls for more and more troops to fight reduced the Monterrey garrison until one day Chavelinos found himself the only officer left in the town. When news reached them the General who'd commanded the Monterrey area was dead Chavelinos took on himself duties, rank and pay of the decased General.

He stood now resplendent in the poorly fitting uniform, the original general having been a slightly smaller man, looking at the money entrusted to him for the purchase of the rifles. Fifty-seven thousand dollars was a lot of money.

"Captain Gonzales!"

Chavelino's shout brought a fat, bewildered looking little man running from another room. Gonzales was a clerk whose original rank of sergeant had been no more than a tribute to his ability to cook books and hide details of bribes received. He was not a fighting man, nor were any of Chavelinos' garrison. The soldiers under him were not the hardy, free-riding vaqueros or the savage, murderous ex-bandidos but poor peons from the agricultural provinces.

"You want me, Terenico?"

Chavelino's face creased in a sudden scowl. "How many times must I tell you to call me General?" he bellowed. "Are the men with rifles here?"

"Yes, but they have placed all their stores in the old cantina."

"How many men left?"

Gonzales gulped worriedly. He had left the finding out of

such details to one of his men and the man failed to bring any report.

"Only four," Gonzales guessed.

"Are you sure? I heard that the Irishman, Conway, left with all his men."

"I meant three."

"Good, then take six men and arrest them."

Gonzales gulped. He was well aware that the men who were in the cantina were well armed and his few meetings with *Americanos del Norte* did not lead him to believe they would surrender mildly to any man. He paused instead of leaping to obey as a good soldier should.

"How?" he asked.

"How!" Chavelinos roared back. "How? Get down there, and demand they surrender to you."

"But what if they won't?"

There Chavelinos could see his Captain had a good point. The General was all too aware of the fighting ability of his men. They would never face up to even three gringos armed with repeating rifles. This was a time for strategy of the highest order.

"I will go down there and talk to these men, and while I am talking you will take your men round the back of the building, enter by the rear window and take command of the room."

Gonzales was far from pleased with this arrangement for he could foresee all kinds of complications ahead of him. However when he tried to raise an argument Chavelinos sniffed and remarked that it would be done or the six men would march under a new Captain and Private Gonzales would be one of the six.

Chavelinos strode importantly through the streets of the town. He would have liked to ride up on his horse but it was a worn out beast left behind as unsuited for hard work. However a small thing like a horse was not important, with the money for the rifles he would be able to take his pick of the finest horses in all Mexico.

His escort straggled behind him and came to a ragged halt in the plaza. The local population fell back before the Commander of their Garrison, the man who was responsible for protecting them from the French. Chavelinos looked at the three men who lounged outside the building, two looked like typical hard-case Texas cowhands, the other, though not Texan, was tough enough too. Each man stood leaning against the wall and each held a rifle on the crook of his arm.

"Who is the one I would talk with?" Chavelinos took in the giant spread of Mark Counter's shoulders and then passed over the small, insignificant looking man in the centre, then halting his gaze on Alden.

"I am," Tom Alden replied. "The rifles are in the cantina here and there they remain until I have the money for them. You have the money?"

"I have the money but I am not satisfied that all is well. You say you have the rifles and your company boasts much about these rifles. I would like to see them work before I make any decisions.

"I would like to see the money here before I waste any of my Company's good ammunition."

"Senor!" Chavelinos's voice was brittle and hard. "I am the General commanding this district. At my command I have three hundred men and can call on every man in Monterrey to help me. It does not pay to take so high a hand with one who can raise such an army."

"These rifles are equal to even an army," Alden replied as he hefted the Henry rifle across his arm.

Behind the cantina Gonzales darted forward on shaky legs followed by six scared looking soldiers. Fear is contagious and the men had caught it from their leader. It was a very worried group who sneaked towards the back of the cantina watching the windows and prepared to make a hurried retreat. At the last house beyond the cantina Gonzales halted his men, confused ideas of military procedure coming to him.

The man gulped and turned to bolt but Gonzales caught him by the coat collar and held him. For a moment the bold Captain thought of whipping out his old horse pistol and shooting the man. It was at that moment he realised that any shot would warn the men out front of the cantina that all was not well. Also Gonzales could not remember if the weapon was loaded or not.

"Advance, all of you," Gonzales waved a hand, but his men made no attempt to move until he started forward himself.

A series of shots from the front of the building brought them all to a halt and there was an air more like startled rabbits than fierce soldiers about them. However, the rear of the cantina remained silent and showed no sign of life so Gonzales started forward again.

In front of the cantina Chavelinos stood looking at the three men, then he snapped, "I want those rifles delivered to the barracks."

"When we are paid," Alden's voice was even.

Dusty was watching the men behind Chavelinos, reading their faces and seeing that they were nervous. Looking down Dusty saw an empty old can laying on the sidewalk, stepped forward, bent and took up the can, threw it into the centre of the street shouting, "Mark!"

Mark brought the new model Henry rifle up to his shoulder, lining and firing fast. The bullets made a rolling tattoo of sound, dust and dirt erupted under the can as it leapt and bounced in the air.

The watching Mexicans stared at the rifle which seemed to pour out a never ending series of bullets, making the can leap and dance. The soldiers drew back slightly, their single shot, awkward old muzzle-loaders hanging heavily in their hands. Every man of the Mexican troops realised how long it took them to reload after a single shot from their muskets and they did not relish facing up to those rapid shooting rifles.

Dusty waited until the shooting ended and then smiled at Chavelinos. It was the hard smile of a man who held four aces dealt pat to him.

"You see, señor, the rifles are as good as Señor Alden claims. There are a thousand inside there. We only have a few of them loaded ready but it will not take long to load more—if we need them."

Chavelinos could almost feel the fear among his men who

realised that for some reason their General was trying to force
the Americanos to give up the rifles without payment. He
heard someone moving about in the cantina and grinned back
at Dusty.

"You have five seconds to surrender to me. Inside the
cantina are my men."

Gonzales, reluctantly, was the first to reach the window.
He was shaking with anxiety but could not see anything.
There was something moving in the cantina. Then he heard
the snort of a horse and realised what had happened. The men
had taken their horses inside the building in case of trouble.

Raising his head with the scared eyes rolling Gonzales
looking in through the window at four horses. Four! There
were only three men outside the cantina and yet there were
four saddled horses there.

Then Gonzales stiffened, his face turning almost ashy
white as he stared at something which was placed directly in
his view. Something which he recognised for what it was
immediately.

"Saludos Manuel," the Ysabel Kid greeted, resting the
muzzle of his old Dragoon gun so that it enveloped the tip of
Gonzales's nose.

Gonzales stood very still. That voice was soft, gentle as a
cooing dove but the mocking, Indian dark face behind was
neither soft nor gentle. Nor were the red hazel eyes soft and
gentle. Gonzales knew who this innocent looking young man
was although he would never regard the Ysabel Kid as either
young or innocent.

"You got other men with you?" the Kid went on.

Never a hero Gonzales nodded weakly and mumbled
"Yes."

"Climb in."

Gonzales climbed. He was never one to refuse a polite
request, much less so when it was delivered by the Ysabel
Kid. There might have been people in Mexico who did not
know *el Cabrito* or who regarded him as a sweet, gentle and
kind young man with a healthy regard for human life. If there
were Gonzales was not one of that number. He knew any

man who disobeyed the Ysabel Kid when that mocking sardonic note was in his voice would get hurt and hurt badly.

The other six men were not aware that anything was wrong. They were all giving their full attention to getting away from here as fast as they could. Not one of them ever gave any thought to their leader talking to an apparently empty room for the Kid held his voice down and the other men had not heard him.

With much grunting and heaving Gonzales climbed through the window and the first of his men was about to follow, being shoved along by the others. All must be all right inside or Gonzales would never have chanced going in there.

The Kid lunged into view with a deep snarl rumbling from his throat. The man gave a yell and lunged backwards crashing into the others. They scattered and there was a mad rush to get away from here.

"How goes it, Manuel?" the Kid asked, knowing Gonzales spoke enough English to get by. Enough to ask for bribes when smuggling was in the air. "Say, you done got yourself all promoted. Like I allus said you can't keep a good man down."

Gonzales licked his lips. He was very scared now. That voice was so soft and friendly that it made him wonder what was coming next. "I came to take charge of the rifles," he said pompously although he felt far from pompous for here was no frightened peon overawed by the importance of an Army uniform.

"Did you now?" the Kid look worried. "Well I can't let you have them. See ole Dusty he told me not to let anyone have them and I couldn't go against him. Now could I? Not with him being my boss and all."

"It is very awkward, Cabrito."

"Why sure. Come on out and meet Dusty." It was a command, not a request.

Outside the cantina Chavelinos looked at the three men in triumph. He could afford to smile. When Gonzales and his men came out of that door he would not only own the rifles but the money which should be paid over for them. Then to make sure there would be no talking the three Americanos would be shot while trying to escape. It was all very convenient.

The three men did not look alarmed; they did not even make any attempt to check on the safety of the building behind them. Dusty knew what was going on in Chavelinos's head and was grinning inside at the shock which was coming to the Mexican general.

"Do you surrender?" Chavelinos asked, watching the shape of Gonzales approaching the doors and the dark form following him.

"Can't," Dusty answered.

"Remember the Alamo," Mark seconded.

"You may remember what you like," Chavelinos answered. "Raise your hands, my men are—!"

The words died off as Gonzales came from out of the cantina followed by not six armed and alert soldiers but one armed and alert gringo. Further a gringo Chavelinos knew all too well.

"What is this, Captain Gonzales?" Chavelinos snarled.

"Ole Manuel here come round the back, just like you figgered, Dusty," the Kid remarked. "I talked him out of it. Allus was a good talker wasn't I Terencio?" the Kid ignored Chavelinos's angry snarls and went on. "Remember one time I got arrested. In court I starts to talk and the judge was clear convinced."

"What happened, Lon?" Alden asked without looking round.

"Sheriff that arrested me got three years in jail."

"You must be a real good talker."

"Either that or 'cause the judge was my uncle."

Dusty cut in on the Kid's flow of memories. "All right, General. What was you saying about us surrendering to you?"

"I want those rifles. Señor Alden you come here in the company of a known criminal and take this high hand with me. Threaten my men—"

"Didn't threaten anybody," the Kid objected. "I just asked old Manuel in for a friendly talk."

"Shut your mouth!" Chavelinos roared. "Señor Alden, I won't ask again for the rifles. I will leave you one hour then I will return and you will either give me the guns or I will take them."

"Bring the money or don't come at all," Alden replied.

Chavelinos snarled something in rapid Spanish, far too rapid for three of the watching men to catch what he was saying to his men. Then he turned and walked off through the crowd followed by Gonzales who was talking a blue streak and waving his hands about as he tried to explain away how the Ysabel Kid had caught him.

"Reckon he'll try anything, Dusty?" Mark was catching the habit of asking Dusty for any advice he needed.

"Might, but he'll have a real hard time getting those peons to follow him. They're real scared of those rifles."

"Sure, they're real scared of the rifles," the Kid agreed. "But he'll come back again. Only this time he's going to bring him a cannon.

CHAPTER THIRTEEN

Kraus Meets A Friend

"RECKON he'll do it, Lon?" Dusty asked as the crowd scattered and cleared away from the area, leaving the plaza open and empty.

"Sure he's not bluffing. We've done got him so crazy wild and mean that he'll do it all right."

"This place won't stand up to a cannon," Alden remarked looking at the thin walls of the cantina.

"Nope and it'll outrange our rifles," Mark went on, "unless we get out of here and fight him along the street. Two of us might be able to get down there and in one of the houses."

"Sure, always allowing that Chavelinos brings his cannon from the direction the two go in." Dusty, strategist as always was thinking faster than the others and had already discarded the same idea. "We don't know where he will bring the cannon in, likely be the easy way and the one that'll give his men the least trouble. But I don't see Chavelinos as a complete fool; he'll have more than enough men to guard that ole cannon. Besides we need at least three men in the cantina to guard it right."

The others could see that Dusty was right, there would be no chance with so small a force against a whole town and a cannon. Dusty was no longer contemptuous of Mexicans as fighting men and knew that even the mildest of men could be roused by fear. Those townsmen were not as a rule fighters, nor were the peons in Chavelinos' force but pushed far enough they would fight. A full-out fight with the people of the town was something none of the men wanted for all knew it would weaken their bargaining power with Juarez and might even lead to the loss of the rifles. Dusty was angry, boiling inside. After all the dangers bringing the weapons here, his mission was endangered by a greedy Mexican officer trying to hold the money for his own use.

"He might not risk using the cannon; it would destroy the rifles," Alden remarked looking at the others.

"Wouldn't do us a whole heap of good neither," the Kid answered. "No Tom, he'll use it. See we've made him lose face in front of the town and he can't let that get by, and keep his rank. He'll use that cannon now even if it means wrecking every rifle in here and to hell with the consequences."

Dusty shrugged. There was little they could do now but wait. There was no chance of getting away with the rifles even if they'd got mules along, not with the Mexican soldiers watching the house from along the street. There was only one thing to do; wait.

The hour dragged by slowly. Dusty set the others to loading reserve rifles ready for use. He was relying on the gunners being as poorly trained as the other men under Chavelinos. He and the other three would lay on the floor while the firing was on and hope for the best. Then if they were alive at the end of the shelling they would come up and start shooting at the advancing soldiers.

"They're coming now, Dusty," the Ysabel Kid might have been pointing out the guests coming into a turkey shoot for all the emotion he showed.

Dusty, Mark and Alden crossed to the window, flattening against the wall and looking out. Chavelinos was bringing all his men along the street and they fanned out moving with if not military precision at least some definite purpose. The men halted around the edge of the plaza and then from the street leading to the barracks came the cannon.

It was an ancient, muzzle loading brass cannon which looked as if it might have been stolen from some privateer long before the Texas War of Independence. It was a museum piece but it would still outshoot the rifles and could send a ball through these walls as if they weren't there at all.

The men with the gun were not as fast or efficient as a trained Yankee artillery group but they still handled the cannon as if they knew what they were doing. Each man took his place quickly enough. The limber was unhooked and the heavy old muzzle turned to face the cantina, then the men loaded it.

"We'd best go out and talk, Tom," Dusty said. "Lon, you and Mark stay in here and cover the back."

Chavelinos stalked forward, halted across the square from the cantina and looked at the two men who stood in front of the building. Then he waved a hand to the men who were in position and towards the cannon along the street.

"You see I am prepared to enforce my commands."

"I see!"

The voice, speaking Spanish came not from the two Americanos but from the door of a store. A small man wearing sober black clothes and with a low crowned black hat on his head stepped out.

"Benito!" Chavelinos gasped; then the streets were swarming with Mexican soldiers.

Not the half-trained peons of Chavelinos, but smart, efficient looking men of the 18th Rancheros. They came from the places where they'd been hiding for half an hour or more. Moving forward they forced back the Chavelinos men, and watching peons and townspeople. Three of them went to the cannon, pushing aside the crew then doused the slow match the leading gunner held. Then on orders the gunners gripped the trails of the gun and turned it away from the cantina. In fifteen seconds these newcomers were in full control of the situation.

"Benito!" Chavelinos' face was grey with fear now. "I can explain what I was doing—"

Two of the Rancheros moved in, one on either side of the shaking man and led him away around the side of a building. Juarez himself stepped forward, holding out a hand to Tom

Alden.

"Señor, I deeply regret what has happened to you since your arrival—" the words were interrupted by a couple of shots, "here. It was none of my doing."

"What was the shooting?" Alden asked.

The Ysabel Kid and Mark Counter were at the door of the cantina now. It was the former young gentleman who stepped forward and replied. Baring his head and raising pious eyes to the heavens he said:

"Poor ole Terencio. He wasn't a bad hombre, just stupid."

By which Alden took it that *ley feuga*, shot while trying to escape had been done on poor Terencio and that his badness or his folly was curbed for good and all.

Juarez's seamed face with the smouldering, fierce black eyes turned next to the fat Gonzales who was trying to hide from view. A brown hand shot out, pointing at the cowering fat man.

"Take the Captain also."

"Now hold on there señor," the Ysabel Kid turned to Juarez. "There's no call to give him *ley feuga*. He was only obeying his orders. Anyway if you shoot him it'll take your men a year to square up his book work."

Juarez looked at the Indian dark young Tejano and smiled a rare flickering smile. "I take your word for it, señor. We have need of good equipment sergeants in the Army and I think Captain Gonzales would be happy back in his old place."

Gonzales turned and headed for the barracks, shedding his Captain's coat as he went. Juarez and the others watched him go then the leader of the Mexican people turned to Alden.

"Now, señor, we can get down to business. I have sent for the money and when it comes you can turn the weapons over to me. Is that one of the rifles?"

"This is the new improved Henry," Alden answered glancing down at his rifle. "The others are of the standard Henry. We had not produced many of this pattern before I left but I brought several for members of your staff. Your men can take the rifles now, señor. I know the money is safe.''

Dusty saw a tall man cross the street towards him, a man as tall and wide shouldered as Mark though some three or four years older. He was no Mexican even though his skin was tanned. His hat was a top quality J.B. Stetson, brown and low crowned. He was handsome and lithe, dressed in a buckskin shirt, blue jeans and wearing a low tied Colt 1860 Army revolver at his right and a knife at his left.

"Cap'n Fog?'' he asked halting in front of Dusty.

"That's me.''

"The name's Bodie, Cheyenne Bodie. I was supposed to meet you in Brownsville but I got delayed on the way down and you'd pulled out when I arrived.''

Dusty took the offered hand, then introduced Mark and the Ysabel Kid. With the formalities completed Dusty got down to business. Alden was talking to Juarez explaining the points of the new Henry rifle and trying to work out another big sale and the soldiers were busy.

"Have you talked with Juarez, Cheyenne?''

"Sure. Some of his men don't like the idea but Juarez agreed. He'll give General Sheldon unrestricted passage to the Texas Line.''

"Sorry I didn't wait on for you up in Brownsville but I saw a chance of having a lever with Juarez if I helped get these rifles here and came down. General Handiman didn't know who would be coming and I wasn't even sure if anyone'd come.''

"It's a good thing you came, Dusty. Gave me something to tell Benito, he wasn't too pleased about the idea of letting Sheldon's men get by him at first.''

The rifles and ammunition were being brought out of the cantina now. The men of the 18th Rancheros examining the wonderful fifteen shot repeaters which would give them such an advantage over the French. The fact that they helped with the carrying out showed their interest for the Rancheros were usually too proud to perform any such menial task as that.

Juarez stood with a finely engraved, silver decorated presentation rifle in his hands. Three of the original thirteen new model Henry rifles were not present. Dusty, Mark and the Kid could have told where they were for each now owned one, Dusty's being one of the pair of carbines Alden had brought.

"Have any trouble getting down here?" the Kid asked Cheyenne.

"Not getting to Juarez. I met him once before and he remembered me. I met him while he was in camp in the hills and the first night I was there a Mexican came to the tent. He'd got a Derringer in his hand when he came in. I woke up and saw him there and when he got near enough he tried to use a knife on me."

"Why?" Dusty had been listening to the talk, now he turned and gave his full attention to the tall man.

"I don't know. I hit the ground out of bed as soon as I saw the knife and shot him. Tried to wound him but the light wasn't good and I killed him. He said something as he came in but spoke so quietly that I couldn't make out what he said."

"What happened to the Derringer?"

"I kept it. Always wanted one of them. Juarez thinks the man was a thief. He didn't belong to the camp. I asked around and none of the men seemed to know him. I don't know why he had the Derringer. It wasn't loaded or even capped."

"Like to see it if I can," Dusty said slowly, but his eyes were glowing in eagerness now.

Cheyenne took the small, singleshot, muzzle loading pistol from his pocket. The Ysabel Kid said something softly as his eyes took in the familiar shape. He reached out and before Dusty could get the gun took it and turned it over to look at it. Under the triggerguard were the scratched letters he'd been expecting. His face showed no expression as he passed the Derringer on to Dusty.

"Did you load it yet, Cheyenne?" Dusty asked.

"No, I've got no mould for it. I aimed to have one made when I got north."

That was what Dusty hoped. He knew that there was so

much variation in the calibre of the hand-made Derringers that each had its own mould and no two were alike. Before Cheyenne could use this Derringer he would have to take it north to a gunsmith and have the mould made for it.

Reversing the gun Dusty opened the small, shield shaped metal plate which covered a cavity in the butt. This was where the percussion caps were kept. No caps were in it now. Only a tight folded sheet of paper which Dusty eased out and unfolded. The message on the paper was written in French and Dusty read it for he could read French even better than he spoke it.

"What's it say, Dusty?" the Kid asked for he could tell his small friend was more than ordinarily interested in the message.

"Something that might interest Juarez. He's going to be killed."

"What do you mean, Dusty?" Mark asked before the other two could speak.

"This letter is for Kraus from Maximillian's second-in-command. He says that Kraus must kill Juarez. That was why the message was hidden in the Derringer. They wouldn't want the man who brought it to know what he was doing. He was a renegade but he was Mexican and he might talk."

"Why'd he come to me?" Cheyenne asked.

"That's got me beat. Where did you sleep that night?"

"Juarez put me in one of his scout's tents. The man was away and not expected back until the next morning."

"He say who the man was?"

"Sure, Kraus, his top-hand scout."

Dusty could see it all now. "You were in Kraus's tent and the man came in with the Derringer in his hand. He thought you were Kraus and then when he saw you weren't spooked and thought it was a trap. The Derringer wasn't loaded so he tried to use a knife."

"That's the way I see it," Cheyenne agreed. "What do we do now?"

"Tell Juarez."

The other three men agreed this was their best bet and went to where Alden was talking with the Mexican leader and his staff. Dusty went up to them with the Derringer and note in his hand. Alden turned with a smile to Juarez and said, "I'd like you to meet Captain Dusty Fog. Without his very able assistance my mission would have failed and the rifles never arrived."

Juarez shook hands with Dusty, then looked down at the Derringer and the sheet of paper. Dusty explained about them and although Juarez knew about Cheyenne shooting the man did not know about the Derringer. He took the sheet of paper and looked it over, then shook his head.

"I do not understand it. I believe it is in French."

"It is," Dusty agreed. "The man Cheyenne killed was taking it to Kraus."

"Kraus?" Juarez's face showed his lack of comprehension. "But Charles Kraus is one of my men and has ridden many times as my scout."

"Ask one of your men to read it for you, or if they can't let Tom here read it," Dusty suggested.

None of the men with Juarez could read French so Alden took the note. He read it through to himself first then told Juarez what the message said. For a moment the Mexican leader was silent. He did not know if he should believe what the Texan was telling him. Yet there was no reason why the man should lie.

"Why should Kraus want to kill me?" he asked.

"Strategy. The French know these rifles are coming, even if they don't know how far ahead we are. So they want to get rid of you. Without Juarez the Mexican people would be leaderless and be easy meat," Dusty answered.

"And because Kraus is a double-dealing rat who'd murder his own mother if there was profit in it," the Ysabel Kid put in, his voice hard and angry. "He and Joe Giss were working together, playing off one side against the other."

Juarez looked at this black dressed Tejano who looked like a boy and spoke fluent, accentless Spanish. He'd heard much of *el Cabrito* and his own Indian blood could spot the wild

Comanche streak in the Ysabel Kid. However Juarez was not satisfied with just that.

"I don't understand what this is all about."

"The man Cheyenne killed was carrying this Derringer and yet tried to use a knife. Cheyenne was in Kraus's tent. The man thought it was Kraus and was going to hand the Derringer over with the message in the cap box. Then when he saw his mistake he got scared and tried to kill Cheyenne."

Juarez watched Dusty all the time the small Texan was speaking. He thought for a moment then asked, "Why would Kraus take orders from the French?"

"His partner's riding with them," the Kid answered. "Joe Giss."

"You appear to know them?"

"They killed my father."

"Then you seek Kraus for revenge?" Juarez looked at the Kid.

"Wouldn't you?"

"I would. And what of Giss?"

"He's dead. I met up with him when he was riding with a French patrol at Santa Juanita."

Juarez shook his head. "This is a matter that takes much thinking about. I owe Cheyenne Bodie my life for he saved it once. I trust him and I also trust Kraus for he has never failed me yet."

"How about when the French nearly got Almonte and Bonaventura?" the Kid asked.

Juarez looked thoughtful. It was a hotly debated point amongst his men how the two *guerillo* leaders had nearly fallen into a French trap. There had been a lot of mistrust and suspicion caused over the incident and Kraus came in for his share of it although nothing had been proved.

"I do not wish to doubt your word about the message," Juarez said thoughtfully, looking at Dusty. "It is that I would wish to be sure before I act."

"There's one way to make sure," Dusty replied.

Kraus rode into Monterrey just after dark and found fiesta reigned in the old town. From the celebrations going on he guessed the rifles were here and from the number of men of the 18th Rancheros knew Juarez was in town. The arrival of the rifles worried him more than a little for he knew that the thousand repeaters could possibly sway the delicate balance of power between the two factions. This was a matter of careful consideration for he wanted to have enough time to warn his partner to get away from the French if their defeat was imminent. It was several days since he last heard from Giss and wondered why. Usually they passed messages every two or three days.

Riding his big black through the town Kraus watched the celebrations with a disinterested eye. There was dancing and excited groups around them celebrating. However it was for the barracks Kraus headed. There he would find Juarez. There also he would find one of Giss's renegades with a message from the French. The man was supposed to have met Giss two days before at the Juarez camp. A French patrol spoiled the arrangements by chasing Kraus and his men off to the south. He'd only just managed to arrive here at Monterrey and his patrol were far behind him.

They made an oddly assorted pair, he and Giss. Where that latter had been tall, lean, illiterate and uncouth Kraus was a short, heavily built, cheerful looking man with some education. It was odd they'd ever become partners but each found in the other an ideal bunkie, alike in ruthless lack of scruples.

The barracks were just as gay as the town and there was quite a celebration going on there. The enlisted men were gathered round a huge fire where a steer was being turned on a spit. All eyes were on a shapely, graceful girl dancing. Kraus halted his horse for a minute, eyeing the girl, approvingly. She was something to look at, lithe, shapely, graceful and very beautiful. After seeing Juarez, Kraus would be back and the girl would be very friendly to a man who stood so high in the affections of Benito Juarez.

Riding on again Kraus flashed a look at the well lit officers' quarters. He guessed there would be a celebration there and doubtless the girl would dance for the top brass later. Then Kraus got an uneasy feeling. His every instinct warned him that unfriendly eyes were watching him. It was the instinct that lay under the hide of every man who rode dangerous trails and one that Kraus would never ignore. From his place in the saddle he turned and looked around, seeing over the heads of the crowd. Yet all he could see were happy, laughing faces, none of the crowd were even taking any notice of him. He tried to shake off the feeling but could not and was still worrying over it when he rode into the stables to leave his horse.

In an upstairs room of the officers' block the Ysabel Kid looked down over the festive scene below him. His red hazel eyes glowed as he watched the second of the men riding by. Kraus was still wearing his knife, the Kid noted with interest. That was good, for Kraus claimed to be some hand with a knife and the Ysabel Kid wanted no advantage.

"That him, Lon?" Mark Counter asked, standing by the Kid's side.

"That's him," the Kid's voice was that deep-throated Comanche grunt as his right hand went across to caress the ivory hilt of his bowie knife.

"Easy boy," Mark warned. "You've got to do it Dusty's way."

"Sure, I don't like doing it but I will."

"It's for the best. Juarez can't read the letter and Dusty wants to show him Kraus isn't loyal. This is the only way we can get proof; then you can have Kraus."

"Sure," the kid's face was that hard Comanche mask again. "Then I can have him."

The Ysabel Kid was more Comanche than ever now.

Kraus was almost over the worried feeling as he walked towards the officers' quarters and inside went straight to the large dining-room. He could hear the laughter and talking from the room and on opening the door found the officers of the 18th Rancheros were being entertained by the Juarez staff.

The long table was flanked by men in uniform and at the head sat Juarez. On either side of Juarez sat two Americans. Kraus studied these four with some caution for he was never truly happy with *Americanos del Norte*. He took in the cowhand dress of the two big men who sat on either side, then studied Tom Alden's eastern clothes. Then he glanced at the small man who sat at Juarez's right hand and wondered what so insignificant a young man was doing there.

The officers of the regiment and some of the Juarez staff shot hostile looks at Kraus as he walked along by them but he was used to that. They resented both his reputation and his attitude towards them.

"Charles, come and meet Mr. Alden who brought the rifles for us," Juarez called.

Kraus went along the table and held out his hand to Alden. Then he was introduced to the other three men. He looked with renewed interest at Dusty Fog and knew now why he sat in a place of honour.

One of the officers sitting next to Cheyenne Bodie pushed back his chair and made room for Kraus to sit down. Then Cheyenne started to bring Dusty Fog's plan into operation.

"Say Kraus. I had a Mexican come looking for you a couple of nights back. You'd best tell him to speak before he comes into a tent in the dark. I near to killed him. He left a Derringer for you.

Kraus's face showed some worry as he looked at the small, heavy calibre gun in Cheyenne's big hand. He was not sure what to reply and felt vaguely uneasy. It was not like one of Giss's men to make a fool mistake like that.

"Say," Dusty put in before Kraus could either say or do anything. "Is that a genuine Henry Derringer gun or one of the copies."

Cheyenne examined the gun, looking at the engraved name on top of the barrel. "The real thing. Got the maker's name on it."

Dusty accepted the gun and turned to Juarez. "You know, señor, they say the Derringer isn't accurate over six feet. I once saw a man killed at fifty yards with one."

"Fifty yards?" Mark put in, like Dusty speaking Spanish. "You must have been drinking Taos Lightning when you saw it."

There was a rumble of agreement from round the table for all the men here knew the Derringer to be a short range weapon.

"Fifty yards, we measured it out later," Dusty stated.

"That's a long shot for one of these," Cheyenne Bodie remarked. "I bet it wouldn't carry the length of this room."

At the word bet the attention of every man in the room was focused on the gun for the Mexican is an avid gambler. In seconds many bets were being made on the subject.

"Like to use your gun to settle this, friend," Dusty said, watching the sweat running down Kraus's face. He glanced in the barrel as if to check on the Derringer being charged.

Before Kraus could either object or agree Dusty was lining the small gun on the wall at the end of the room. He eased back the hammer and pressed the trigger. A dry click rewarded his efforts and Dusty looked down at the gun, drew back the hammer and remarked, "No cap."

Kraus licked his lips, then growled, "Give me the gun back. I've got another in my saddlebag that you can use."

"No need to waste that much time. I'll just get a cap out of the box here."

Kraus lunged forward as Dusty started to raise the cover of the butt box cap. He knew that there would be a message in there and who it would be from for he recognised the Derringer as one he'd left not with Giss but with Maximillian's second-in-command. Whatever the message was it would never do for Juarez to see it.

"Give it here," he snarled. "I don't like folks messing with my gun."

"Charles," Juarez spoke softly, his eyes on the other man's face. "I also have laid wagers. I would like to see them decided right away. Let us settle the wagers now."

"There's no caps in the box." Kraus answered, his eyes flickering around the room.

Dusty stood up and moved round his chair slightly. "How'd you know that? You haven't looked."

Juarez still kept his eyes on Kraus's face and saw the guilty look in them. He knew that Dusty told the truth. Kraus was a traitor and the message was genuine from the French.

"Take the gun and look in the cap box," he snapped.

Kraus's hand dropped towards the gun at his side and at the same moment Dusty moved faster than a striking diamondback. He hurled forward, arms locking round Kraus's legs and lifting. Taken by surprise by Dusty's tackle Kraus was lifted clear off his feet and brought crashing down on to the ground. His Navy Colt slid from its holster and he clawed desperately for it.

A foot came down hard on to Kraus's hand pinning it within inches of the gun-butt. Kraus's eyes went to the boot, then up over the black trousers. Fear hit him when he saw that butt-forward old Dragoon gun, then the black shirt and bandana. Then to the dark face with the cold red hazel eyes.

"Howdy Charlie," the Ysabel Kid's voice was gentle and caressing. "I've been waiting to see you for a piece now."

CHAPTER FOURTEEN

Bush Sheldon's Decision

KRAUS looked up at the expressionless face of the Ysabel Kid as the dark young man moved slowly backwards and let him come to his feet. There was murder in Kraus's eyes but his lips still held a friendly smile that had disarmed and made unsuspicious several men.

"Howdy Lon. Looks like the end of the trail for me. I'm sorry about your father but there was no other way."

"It was a fool mistake, Charlie."

The other men in the room were all silent, watching the final act in a drama which started just south of the Rio Grande and was being brought to an end here. Not one of the men would make any move to interfere for every man here knew of the feud between Kraus and the Ysabel Kid. It was for the Kid to make the next move, or for Kraus.

"We made it pay for a spell, Lon. Got a fair sum cached out in case we ever needed to light out fast. Reckon you know Giss'll be looking for you?"

"Giss's dead. Met up with him at Santa Juanita and I got your other boys."

Kraus nodded; he'd guessed as much. There was nothing hurried in the way he moved but he was measuring the distance between them with calculating eyes. All too well he knew what little chance he would stand in a fair fight with the Ysabel Kid. He'd seen that Comanche brand of knife work too often to believe he could hope to match it. His right hand dipped into his pocket and lifted out a sack of Bull Durham.

"Mind if I roll a smoke first?" he asked.

The left hand brought out the knife fast and threw it across his body to be caught in the right as the sack of tobacco fell to the floor. In the same move Kraus lunged in, the blade of his knife ripping up a savage drive for the Ysabel Kid's bowels. It was a brutal stroke, sent with the full weight of Kraus's body behind it as he lunged in to get his muscular frame behind the blow. It was a move he'd perfected and used on three occasions with some considerable success.

Against a white man it would have succeeded but at that moment the Ysabel Kid was pure Comanche and he moved with Indian speed. His left arm slashed across to deflect the knife holding arm to one side. Kraus's weight carried him forward and as he did he felt the Kid's left hand catch his arm and spin him. Then the great bowie knife in the Ysabel Kid's trained right hand made a shinning arc. Full to the hilt it sank in the stomach, the target of the knife fighter. It sank in and ripped up. Kraus let his knife fall through his fingers as the terrible pain of the wound ripped through him. His hand clawed at the gaping wound as if trying to stop the flow of blood. Then he went down on the floor.

The Kid stepped back, his face the face of a Comanche Dog Soldier who has counted coup. Then the red fire died in his eyes and he became once more the baby faced innocent looking young man who'd captured hearts from señoritas all over Mexico.

"Sorry I mussed up your floor, señor," he said to Juarez.

Three days later Dusty Fog brought his two friends to a halt. They were getting near to Saltillo now, the place where they would find General Bushrod Sheldon.

"Time we got into uniform, I reckon," he said.

"Haven't seen either French or Juaristas, Dusty," Mark pointed out.

"Nope and I hope we don't. But I figger they know we're in Mexico and they are expecting something. We ride in there in cowhand clothes and they'll get all suspicious. But if we ride in uniform they'll maybe take us for a detachment from another fort.''

''Sure there are a few more of us serving, men that didn't come down with ole General Bush. I'll tell them you are one of them.''

''How about me,'' the Kid inquired.

''You've got a uniform in your warbag. You'll wear it,'' Dusty answered.

''Ain't but a private.''

''That's good. You'll be able to get on to the enlisted men and warn them. If they know about us they might recognise that big white of your'n,'' Dusty answered. ''It stands out like a nigger on a snowdrift. Maybe you'd best stay out here.''

''Mebbe hell,'' the Kid growled back. ''You've plumb ruined me as a smuggler by making me go visiting sheriffs so you're going to hold to giving me a riding chore when we've done here.''

''So?''

''So I'm sticking close to you in case you change your mind.''

They headed for a small clump of trees off the main trail and in the shelter hidden from prying eyes they unpacked their uniforms from warbags. The Kid also took a small package out but did not explain what it was.

Mark pulled on his jacket, the sleeve of which had been mended by a woman in Monterrey. He was still wearing his issue trousers, boots and hat, so he was the first changed. He looked at Dusty who was changing into the uniform so carefully packed in his warbag. Mark smiled as he noted the cut of the jacket. Despite his reputation as a strict disciplinarian he flouted dress regulations by wearing a jacket cut in the Counter fashion, the fashion Mark himself was responsible for. Also Dusty did not wear an issue sword belt, retaining his own hand tooled buscadero gunbelt with the matched, bone handled Colt guns in the holsters.

Turning Mark found that the Kid was not even starting to change yet. He'd got the mysterious package open and was rubbing some powder on the sleek white coat of the stallion. Before he'd done his horse was transformed from an all white to a piebald. Then and then only did he get his rather worn private's uniform on.

There was a subtle change in Dusty as he swung into the saddle of the big paint. The easy slough had gone from him now, he sat more erect in the saddle and there was an air about him that was plain to any man who'd ever served under a real tough, efficient officer.

They rode into Saltillo town and passed through the streets attracting no attention from the few Mexicans who were about. The barracks was on the other side of town and as they rode towards it Dusty was sure something was wrong. He halted his horse and looked at the high walls which surrounded the barracks. On either side of the main gate was something which looked both strange and familiar to him.

"Only French sentries," Dusty remarked softly.

"Saw that. Usually we have our own men on the main gate guard."

The three men rode nearer and the French soldier who stood slackly at easy by the gate looked them over without any great interest. He lifted his carbine in a sloppy salute and allowed them through.

Stood facing the gate was the officers' mess and quarters, surrounded by a low adobe wall. To the right of the officers' country lay a line of barrack rooms, to the left a large building which gave all signs of being a mess-hall. From the sounds which came from this building a meal was in progress.

Dusty took this in as he swung down from his paint outside the officers' mess garden wall. Then he glanced up and felt the hair rising on the back of his neck.

"See those two gatlings?" he asked softly.

"Sure, they've been there all the time. Four men crew for them on watch."

"How long have they been trained in this way?"

Mark and the Ysabel Kid, without any due haste or apparent worry turned and glanced up at the wall. The two gatling guns were on naval style swivel mounts instead of the more usual wheeled carriages. They were placed to give covering fire on the streets of the town, but right now they were turned with the muzzles in towards the barracks.

Dusty ran his tongue over his lips. He'd seen a gatling gun in action and knew that it was the most terrible fighting weapon ever invented by man. He looked at the wall, then at the ladder which led up to the walk on the wall side.

"Something stinks, Mark," he whispered.

"Sure." Before Mark could do more than agree he saw a man coming towards him. A squat, wide-shouldered, dark faced man wearing the uniform of a sergeant but with a buscadero gunbelt supporting a brace of matched Colt 1860 Army revolvers in tied down holsters. "Howdy Ben, what's all that up there?"

The sergeant halted and to Mark's surprise came to a smart brace and brought off a salute. "No idea, suh." It was to Dusty he replied. "French relieved us on gate guard duty two days back."

Mark and the Ysabel Kid looked at each other. They both knew that Ben Thompson was not the best soldier in the world and noted for disrespect to officers. Yet he was acting very respectful to Captain Dusty Fog. It was some surprise for although as yet Ben Thompson had not reached fame as one of the fast guns he was still reckoned with as a handy man to have around.

"How many French troops are there here?" Dusty inquired.

"Only about fifty and they stay well clear of us. Spend nigh on all their time in their barrack block down there. We're still bunking in the mess hall."

Dusty glanced first at the barrack block then at the mess hall. Men in the barracks, covered and aided by those gatling guns would have the soldiers in the mess hall under their guns and at their mercy.

"Where's General Sheldon?" Dusty asked.

"In the officers' mess room. Having lunch with the other brass."

"Good. I'm going in there, Lieutenant Counter in fifteen

minutes you, the sergeant here and Private Ysabel will deal with those two gatling gun crews. If you hear a shot from inside do it immediately. If not in fifteen minutes.''

''What's going on?'' Thompson growled.

''Bengeeman, ole friend,'' the Kid replied. ''Don't you go worrying about that. Let's get the hosses out of the way and then do what the Cap'n says. I'll tell you what it's all about.''

Dusty watched the two men lead off the horses and then turned back to Mark. ''It's real important you get those guns, you know that?''

''I know it. They'll be stopped.''

Turning, Mark walked across the open space, the French soldiers paying little or no attention to him as he leaned against the wall near the ladder and started to roll a smoke.

Dusty turned on his heel, pushed open the door of the officers' mess building and entered. He glanced around as he stood in the hall, then removing his hat he crossed to where he could hear sound of men talking. On opening the door he found he'd come to the right place. It was like a scene out of the War. The room and the men in it could have stepped straight out of Georgia for all of them wore the uniform of the Confederate Army. Coloured waiters moved among the dozen or so officers carrying trays. One of them saw Dusty in the doorway and came forward to take his hat but he retained his gunbelt.

General Bushrod Sheldon was seated in a comfortable chair, big, lean and as usual with a cigar stuck between his beared lips. He and the other men looked Dusty over with some interest for they knew he was not one of them. He crossed the room striding smartly in a completely different manner from the usual way he lounged along when not in the saddle. Halting he saluted the General.

''Cap'n Fog of the Texas Light Cavalry with dispatches for General Sheldon from General Grant.''

Bushrod Sheldon looked up, his eyes frosty and cold. ''Is that your idea of a joke, Captain?'' he barked.

''I never joke with my superiors, sir,'' Dusty answered. ''With the General's permission.''

He drew the letter from his jacket front and held it out. Sheldon took it, turning it over in his hands. "What's this all about, Captain?" he asked. "Have you come down here to join us?"

"No sir. To fetch you back home."

"Back! Back did you say. You mean, sir, to stand there and ask me to go back to Georgia and make peace with the Yankees?"

"No sir. For the Yankees to make peace with you. Uncle Devil sent me along to say that he had read the letter and knows it will be honoured."

Sheldon studied Dusty, remembering him now, a small man who'd come into his camp one night with prisoners, two generals, a colonel and three majors taken from a place where they might have thought safe from attack.

"So Ole Devil Hardin sent you along did he?"

"Yes sir, now the letter there—" Dusty held up his hand to stem the angry words unsaid. "A wise Southern gentleman once told me always to look into a proposition then condemn it."

Sheldon coughed. He remembered saying those words one time back before the War whilst on a visit to the Rio Hondo. He opened the envelope and took out the sheet of paper. Every eye was on him as he spread flat the paper and started to read. Every man here was hoping their leader would agree to go north again. By the time he'd reached the third line of the paper Sheldon's face wasn't red and angry any more, instead it was relaxed and thoughtful.

"Is this on the level, Captain Fog?" he asked passing the letter to the Colonel who stood near him.

"They have started to rebuild Sheldvale?"

"Started as soon as I left for Mexico," Dusty answered. That was one of the concessions, that Sheldon's home, Sheldvale, destroyed by the Union Army after the war would be rebuilt. "They will make restitution to any man who suffered loss of his property during the occupation of the South and will accept any officer, noncom or man into the Cavalry with rank and seniority standing."

There was a sudden rush of talk. Every eye was on Sheldon even more now and in every face he read one thing, willingness to leave Mexico and go back home again. Sheldon looked at the last paragraph again. He was to take his old seat in Congress again as soon as he'd been home and straightened out his affairs.

"What does Ole Devil think about all this?"

"He allows it's time you came home and took your share. Likely you didn't hear that he took a bad fall from a hoss and tied down in a wheelchair. That means he can't attend Congress and that leaves it all on General French."

"Very interesting, mon General!"

The men all turned. The door at one side of the big room was open and three French officers stood there. In the centre was a big, fat, heavily moustached colonel, at his right was a short, stocky major and at his left stood Captain Bardot.

The Captain looked leaner and his face was savage for he was still feeling the effect of the long walk back to the nearest French troops. In his hand he held a Lefauchex revolver, lined on Dusty Fog.

"What's all this about, Mornec?" Sheldon barked. "Why is Captain Bardot pointing that gun at Captain Fog?"

"It appears you are entertaining a traitor, General. That will not please my superiors."

"What do you mean traitor?" Sheldon growled, the other officers looking on and ready to follow the leader.

"This is the man who shot Major Harmon in Brownsville and who brought the repeating rifles for Juarez."

Sheldon swung round and fixed his hard eyes on Dusty. "Is that true?"

"Sure. I wanted a lever to get you free, unrestricted passage north from Juarez. Bringing those rifles to him gave me that lever. That way we won't need to fight Mexicans all the way north."

"You were so sure I'd go back with you?"

"I was sure you'd be too sensible to refuse."

Mornec laughed and pointed from the window to the barrack buildings. "I was expecting this and took precautions, even though I was ordered to detach my main force and keep only a skeleton garrison here. My men are stood by ready and the gatling guns cover the entrance of the mess hall. If your men try to get out they will be killed."

"Just as I will kill this one," Bardot hissed and started to lift the revolver he was holding and line it on Dusty.

One of the negro servants dropped the tray he was holding. It clattered to the floor and Bardot glanced towards the sound. His eyes were off Dusty for less than a second but it was long enough. Like a flicker of lightning Dusty's hands moved crossing and bringing out the matched guns. Both roared and Bardot rocked over backwards under the hammering impact of the .44 bullets.

"Stand still, Colonel!" Dusty's command froze Mornec and his Major even as they started to think about drawing their own weapons. "Take their guns one of you gentlemen, please. I don't want to have to kill them."

The sound of the shot was heard outside the walls of the building. It brought the attention of the gatling gun crews from the outside of the fort to the inside.

Mark Counter started up the ladder thanking the inefficiency of the French in that the crews of the guns were not issued with sidearms, not even their short Artillery sabres.

The other gun crew were not so slow in moving. Even as the Ysabel Kid and Ben Thompson came into view the gunner started the weapon swinging round. The Kid brought up his Henry rifle and fired all in one move. The loader of the gun slid down with a hole between his eyes. Before either the Kid or Thompson could make a further move the gun started to chatter. Neither of the Americans wasted any time. They hit the ground behind the small wall around the officers' country, diving over it and hugging the base as the .58 calibre bullets smashed through the air over their heads.

Mark started up the ladder, climbing fast. He was almost level with the top when one of the gatling gun crew saw him. The man ran along the parapet and lifted his foot to kick down at Mark. The Texan let loose of the ladder with his right hand, stabbing it out and catching the down-swinging foot.

From the corner of his eye he saw the French soldiers coming from the barrack building, armed and ready for war. He gripped the foot and twisted it as the man tried to force it down on him and shove both Mark and the ladder backwards. Mark felt himself moved back and tightened his grip on the foot. The Frenchman was dragged nearer the edge and pulled back bringing the ladder to the wall again. Still holding the foot Mark lunged up another step and heaved. The French soldier yelled as he shot forward on one leg; then he was falling.

The man handling the gatling gun saw Mark gain the parapet and started to traverse the gun round. Mark saw the yawning multitude of barrels of the gun swinging round and flung himself flat as the gunner turned the firing handle. The bullets hammered over his head, smashing into the stone of the parapet behind him. Mark's right hand Colt was out even as he dropped and his other hand fanned the hammer. In the next seconds Mark disproved two theories which were to be discussed many times over the years: that a really good man with a gun never fanned the hammer and that no man could be accurate while fanning.

The shots rolled out, sounding almost as fast as the gatling gun chatter. Firing up under the swivel mounting Mark sent two bullets into the lower body of the gunner then as the man staggered back and the thunder of the gatling died away, Mark sent a bullet into one of the other two men. The last man turned and leapt down the twelve foot gap from parapet to ground. He lit down running and almost made it. Who shot him was never discovered for by now the Confederate soldiers and the French were shooting at each other.

Mark came up and holstered the gun. He saw at a glance taken as he leapt for the gatling gun, that his help was needed. The Confederate soldiers were in the worst position, caught out in the open. They were cavalry men and southern cavalry at that. Their weapon was either the sabre or the hand-gun and few had even a carbine, while the French were armed with rifles. Also the gatling gun on the other side of the gate would be turned against them as soon as the menace of the

Ysabel Kid and Ben Thompson was removed. Even now the gatling gun was tearing pieces from the adobe wall they were sheltered behind.

Mark swung the gun round. He knew how to handle it and knocking off the magazine which was on the gun he placed a full one on. Sighting on the other gatling gun he whirled the handle, the barrel turned and the gun chattered throwing lead across the open space.

The second gun crew had not seen what was happening. The first inclination they had that anything was wrong was when lead from their neighbouring gatling hit the wall near them.

The Kid looked up as soon as the firing halted, one glance telling him what was happening. He glanced at Ben Thompson;

"You handle one of those things, Ben?"

"Why sure."

"Let's go then!"

From behind the wall leapt two figures, one with a brace of roaring Colt guns and the other with a crashing Henry rifle. The Kid and Ben Thompson sprinted out across that open space. Their rapid dash attracted attention from the French soldiers but Mark's gatling gun churned out its song and caused a rapid hunting for cover amongst the French who were safely beyond pistol range but well within the area of fire the gatling gun covered.

The crew of the second gatling tried to bring their gun to bear. The Ysabel Kid's rifle cracked and the gunner went down. Ben Thompson threw three fast shots and sent the man who leapt to replace the dead gunner rolling on the parapet. The other man decided on discretion. He ran along the wall, Thompson's Colts cracked out again and slowly as if he was tired the man sank to the ground.

The Kid halted forcing bullets into the loading gate of his rifle and then yelled. "Get up and let her go, Ben."

Thompson went up the ladder fast. Below him the repeating rifle cracked at a rate the French single loaders could never equal and beyond them Mark Counter kept up a flow of fire far beyond anything the rifle could manage.

Under the menace of the two guns the Confederate soldiers advanced fast until some of them at least were in range of the French. Then with both gatling guns ready to chatter out their message and more Confederate men getting into place every minute the French surrendered.

Bushrod Sheldon was the first man from the officer's quarters. He took in the situation at a glance and turned to Colonel Mornec who was standing under escort behind him.

"Colonel, I'm telling my men to prepare to march out. You will be left here with only these few troops. If you're wise you'll get out fast."

Mornec knew this to be the truth. There would be no chance for him with his few men against the Juarez forces. He could see that his force was even more depleted since the fighting started.

"What do you suggest, Colonel?"

"That you leave as soon as you can. We'll allow you to take your arms, not the gatling guns but your small arms. I'd be gone as soon as possible if I were you."

The French Colonel nodded in agreement. He was getting far better treatment than he'd expected. Turning to the major he snapped an order for the men to be ready to march in one hour.

After the French pulled out the bugle sounded assembly and the men buzzing with talk and rumours gathered. Ben Thompson and the Ysabel Kid had been closely questioned by the others and a suspicion of what was going to happen was being passed around.

Silence fell as the men watched their leader coming towards them, General Bushrod Sheldon halted and looked round. They stood before him, the men who'd served under him in the Civil War and the men who'd come in with him when he brought the troops to Mexico. Every man here was known to him, the good soliders, the bad, the indifferent.

"Men," he said. "This is Captain Dusty Fog of the Texas Light Cavalry. He came here to bring me a message from General Grant."

An excited murmur ran through the ranks of men at the words. It was some moments before Sheldon could make himself heard. He remained silent until the men all stopped talking then went on:

"General Grant wants us to return to our homes. He offers us the chance to take up our lives where we left off. To any man who wishes to remain in uniform he offers entry to the cavalry with whatever rank the man holds. To any man who wishes to return home and finds his home destroyed the United States will pay for the home to be rebuilt. To any man who wishes to go west and make a new life financial aid will be given. Now you men have served me well and as of now we are no longer a fighting regiment. The choice is in your hands. Those who wish may ride north with me. Any who don't wish to ride north may go with the French."

A tall gangling sergeant major stepped forward and saluted, then in a slow, easy Kentucky drawl said, "General, sir. We all aims to ride with you but how about the Juaristas. We'll have to fight them all the way and we're a mite low on powder and ball."

"Captain Fog can answer for that," Sheldon replied.

All eyes went to the small man who was a legend among them, a name to rank with Turner Ashby and John Singleton Mosby.

"I came down here with a consignment of repeating rifles for Juarez. In return for that he is giving you unrestricted passage to the border and supplying an escort to make sure nothing goes wrong."

Then the discipline of the regiment went by the boards. Men whooped, yelled and slapped each other on the back.

"Yowee!" Ben Thompson screamed and fired his revolver into the air. "Yowee. Boys, we're going home!"

THE END